replica

Virtual Amy

MARILYN KAYE

BANTAM BOOKS

NEW YORK • TORONTO • LONDON • SYDNEY • AUCKLAND

y

RL5.5, 008–12

VIRTUAL AMY

A Bantam Skylark Book/ December 2001

ISBN 0-553-48749-3

Visit us on the Web! www.randomhouse.com/kids

Published simultaneously in the United States and Canada

Bantam Skylark is an imprint of Random House Children's Books, a division of
Random House, Inc. SKYLARK BOOK and colophon and BANTAM BOOKS
and colophon are registered trademarks of Random House, Inc. Bantam Books,
1540 Broadway, New York, New York 10036.

PRINTED IN THE UNITED STATES OF AMERICA

OPM   10   9   8   7   6   5   4   3   2   1

For Dyan and Riq

Virtual Amy

one

The door to Chris's bedroom was open, but Amy knocked anyway, just to be polite.

There was no response from her friend. The dark-haired boy was at his desk, glaring at his computer and mumbling under his breath. Amy entered the room and stood behind him. She looked over his hunched shoulders.

On the screen, Amy saw a vivid, artistic rendition of a magnificent garden. She could identify yellow daffodils, white daisies, and purple violets. A border of multicolored pansies lined a walkway that meandered around rosebushes and exotic flowers she couldn't name. Marble sculptures dotted the landscape; one was an angel with outstretched arms, another a unicorn. In a corner of the garden stood a lavish fountain, spouting streams of water from different levels. It all looked pretty realistic, although a little too perfect.

The sound effects were good too. Amy heard water splashing in the fountain, wind rustling in the trees, and birds chirping as they occasionally flew across the sky at the top of the screen. It was all very pleasant, but apparently Chris wasn't happy with the scene. He was fiddling with his mouse, sending the cursor all over the place and clicking on everything in sight. Finally, he let out a groan of frustration.

"What's the matter?" Amy asked.

"I can't get away from this garden," Chris complained. "There's got to be a way out, but I don't see it. I can't even find a clue." He frowned. "Maybe I need a password."

Now Amy understood. "You're playing Darklands."

Chris nodded. "I've been stuck in this stupid garden for an hour."

It was next to impossible for Amy to drum up any real sympathy for him in his predicament. Personally, she found Darklands to be less than thrilling. In fact, it bored her silly. She was sick of hearing about it.

Not that she'd ever played much herself. Two or three experiences had taught her that the computer game was enormously frustrating, an utter waste of time, and no fun at all.

That opinion put her in the minority. It seemed as if *everyone*—at least everyone between the ages of twelve and sixteen—was playing Darklands nonstop. Sometimes, Amy thought she was the only thirteen-year-old in the world who was not a member of the Darklands fan club.

Still, for Chris's sake, she tried to fake a little interest. "So you want to leave the garden, huh?"

"Yeah. There's got to be a message somewhere that gives you a clue how to get out."

"Out to where?"

"I'm trying to get to the next level of enlightenment. You see that castle?"

Amy made out a faint image in the corner of the screen. It was the classic fairy-tale castle, with ornate decorations and multiple turrets. The castle was surrounded by a moat. "Yeah, I see it."

"The passage to the next level is through the castle. So I have to get inside it."

"Have you tried clicking on the castle?" Amy asked him.

"Of *course* I clicked on it," Chris said in an aggrieved tone. "Do you think I'm stupid? That's the first thing I

3

tried. I can only get as far as the moat. And there's no boat or bridge to get across the water."

"Maybe you've hit a dead end," she suggested.

"There are no dead ends in Darklands," he informed her. "There's always a way to get from one place to another."

Amy studied the screen. "Can I try something?"

"Sure."

Chris got up and gave Amy his seat. She put her hand on the mouse, moved the cursor around the screen, and clicked at random. Nothing happened. She even clicked on the water in the moat, thinking it might part like the Red Sea, but still nothing happened. Another flock of birds crossed the screen, and that gave her an idea. She moved the cursor and began clicking rapidly.

"What are you doing?" Chris wanted to know.

"I'm trying to click on a bird," she told him, chasing the last bird in the flock with the arrow. "Maybe you can *fly* across the moat."

"It won't work," Chris said. "The birds are just background, you can't access them."

"Oh, well, is there anything else that flies?"

"No . . . wait, give me the mouse." Chris practically shoved Amy out of the chair. "See that angel? Check out her right hand!"

"What about it?"

"Doesn't it look like she's pointing? Yes! She's pointing at those stones!"

"So click on the stones," Amy suggested.

Chris rolled his eyes. "That would be too easy. There's got to be some sort of message in them." He stared at them intently.

Amy couldn't sustain her pretended interest. While Chris studied the stones, she looked around his room. She'd been there several times before, but each time she visited there was something different about it.

It was a nice bedroom, with a green-and-blue plaid bedspread, matching curtains, and a soft blue rug on the floor. It was on the second floor of the house, and the window overlooked a leafy tree. Chris had decorated the walls with posters of the L.A. Lakers and a Brazilian soccer team. There was all the usual stuff—shelves crowded with books and magazines, a phone, a CD player—but she also noticed something new: a small portable TV.

She was impressed. For a foster home, this was excellent.

It hadn't always been like that. When Chris was first sent to live with the Martins, the couple had been nice enough, but they certainly hadn't gone out of their way to make him comfortable. They were distant and formal, and while they provided food and shelter, they didn't show any real interest in the fifteen-year-old boy.

All that had seemed to change about a month ago, just after Chris's unpleasant encounter with his birth father. The Martins warmed up to him. They started giving him stuff, like the computer, the CD player, and now this TV. They wanted to meet his friends, and they encouraged him to invite them to the house. They even went out of their way to get to know his friends' families. Amy's mother and Mrs. Martin now took an aerobics class together three times a week. The once sullen and angry Chris Skinner, the homeless boy who'd been abandoned and betrayed by his real parents, was actually beginning to smile once in a while.

He was smiling at that moment. "I think I've got it."

"What?"

"The clue. See how the stones are grouped? I'll bet there's a pattern to the number of stones in each bunch." He started counting under his breath. "It's a code! I just have to figure out which letter— Whoa!"

There was a sudden eerie whistling sound, followed by a dark shadow that emerged from behind a statue. Looking closely, Amy saw that it was a hooded figure with the face of a skeleton. Chris quickly moved the cursor on it and clicked. The figure let out a muffled scream and exploded.

"Gotcha!" Chris exclaimed happily.

"What was *that*?" Amy asked.

"An Intruder. They live underground in Darklands, and they can obliterate you if you don't stop them first. You have to zap them within five seconds or the entire game collapses around you. Just like that you can be history."

"Gee, that's scary," Amy said. She was being sarcastic, but Chris didn't pick up on that.

"Intruders pop out of nowhere," he went on, "just when you're getting excited about something else and you're not paying attention. The guy who invented this game was smart."

"Oh yeah," Amy said. "A regular genius." This time Chris didn't miss the sarcasm. But he wasn't offended.

"Okay, maybe he wasn't a genetically altered clone with an IQ of two hundred and one. Maybe he was just a regular run-of-the-mill clone like me. But he had to be pretty intelligent to create this game. No one's ever made it to the end."

"There's absolutely nothing run-of-the-mill about you," Amy assured him. "I bet you'll be the first to figure this game out. Just don't spend twenty-four hours a day doing it, okay?"

"Chris! Amy! Dinner's ready!" Mr. Martin's jovial voice rang out from the dining room below. The promise of food tore Chris from Darklands and he and Amy both ran downstairs. The other invited guest was already at the table with Chris's foster father.

"Hi, Mom," Amy greeted Nancy Candler, and blew a kiss in her direction.

"Hi, sweetie," Nancy replied. "Chris, that's a great sweater."

Amy hadn't even noticed the red sweater Chris was wearing, its arms tied carelessly around his neck. "Is that new?" she asked him.

"Yeah. From Mona and Frank." That was what Chris called his foster parents. Mona Martin was coming into the dining room with a steaming platter, and she heard him.

"Are you talking about the sweater?" she asked. Turning to Nancy, she said, "Isn't it nice to see him wearing something besides black?"

"Very nice," Nancy said with approval, and Chris went almost as red as the sweater.

They were certainly showering him with gifts, Amy thought. Probably to make up for Chris's discovery that he was a clone of his so-called father and that he'd been created in case his father needed spare parts. It had been a blow to Chris, and he was still bitter. It helped that Amy, his girlfriend, was also a scientifically created being, and he didn't resent the fact that her altered and refined genes gave her abilities he'd never have.

The steaming platter turned out to be chicken and noodles, a perfect dish for an evening that was cool for Los Angeles. There were rolls and salad to go with it. The adults had wine, Amy and Chris had sparkling water, and everyone happily dug in.

"When are you leaving for Seattle?" Frank Martin asked Nancy.

"Friday morning," Nancy replied.

"And you'll return . . . ?"

"Monday evening. It's just a weekend conference."

"Amy can stay with us while you're gone," Mona Martin suggested.

"Thanks for the offer," Nancy said, "but that won't be necessary. Our neighbor, Monica Jackson, is going to stay at our place."

That was the first Amy had heard of the plan. "How come I'm not staying with Tasha?" she asked. Usually, when her mother went out of town for short trips, Amy stayed next door with her best friend and her family.

"Tasha's mother called this afternoon," Nancy explained. "They've got an unexpected invitation to a ski lodge for the holiday weekend."

Amy knew she'd be hearing plenty of complaints from Tasha about *that*. They'd made plans to watch MTV's *Real World* marathon that weekend. And Tasha liked skiing about as much as she liked most athletic activities—which was to say, not at all.

Eric would be pleased, though. Tasha's brother—and Amy's ex-boyfriend—liked all sports. He played soccer and basketball in high school.

Actually, it was probably just as well that Amy wasn't staying at Tasha's. It was still a little uncomfortable for her to be around Eric. She missed the very special relationship they'd once had. Eric had been the first person to learn Amy's secret—that her mother wasn't really her mother, that Amy had been created in a laboratory by scientists as part of something called Project Crescent, that she was one of thirteen Amys, and that the scientists had disbanded the project when they learned it was funded by an organization intent on creating a master race of superior people. Eric had been with Amy during her early encounters with the organization, and he'd shared some scary experiences with her. It was only natural that they had become boyfriend and girlfriend.

But everything had changed when Eric finished Parkside Middle School and started tenth grade. At least,

Eric had changed. Suddenly, he was full of himself, acting superior, and he never missed an opportunity to put down Amy, Tasha, and any other middle school kids. Amy couldn't take his attitude, and she finally broke up with him. She'd said they could still be friends, but of course, that was easier said than done, and they were still pretty stiff around each other.

Being honest, though, Amy had to admit that it wasn't entirely Eric's fault. He knew all about Andy and what had happened in Paris.

"Hello? Hello? Earth to Amy. Come in, Amy," Chris said.

Amy realized that everyone was looking at her, that her thoughts had kept her out of the conversation. "Sorry," she apologized. "I was daydreaming."

"About what?" Mrs. Martin asked with interest.

Amy had to come up with something fast. "Uh, Monica, our neighbor. She's an artist. She came with Mom and me to Paris last year."

"Another conference," Nancy informed them.

Chris looked at Amy with surprise. "I didn't know you'd been to Paris."

"Yeah, it was fun," Amy said. There were a lot of things Chris didn't know about her yet. Like the fact that there had been another Project Crescent experiment, one that had taken place two years before the project that created the Amys. This earlier experiment in cloning had created males, who were all called Andy. And one of those Andys had been in Paris with her. . . .

Amy forced herself to put aside these private thoughts and concentrated on the dinner conversation. Mr. Martin was telling stories about his job in direct marketing. It had something to do with sales, which Amy didn't really understand, but he was making everyone laugh with his funny impersonations of peculiar clients. Mrs. Martin had made a yummy chocolate mousse for dessert, and all in all, it was a super evening.

The Martin house was close enough for Nancy and Amy to walk home. "I hope you're not too disappointed about the Morgans' taking off for the weekend," Nancy said. "I had to tell them over and over that you wouldn't be upset."

"It's okay," Amy said. "I don't mind. Chris and I will hang out."

"Just make sure Monica always knows where you are," Nancy warned her.

Amy assured her mother that she would inform Monica of her whereabouts, but privately, she had to smile at the thought. Monica was a free spirit, not a baby-sitter. She had been Amy's chaperone in Paris, but Amy had always found it easy to do whatever she wanted there. She didn't expect this weekend would be any different.

"That was nice of the Martins to invite me to stay," she said.

"I'm glad Chris has such pleasant foster parents," her mother said. "He's a fine boy."

Amy certainly agreed. She wasn't sure she'd call Chris her boyfriend, but they had lots of good times together. Tonight had been fun. She hadn't even been hit with one of her headaches.

The headaches she'd been having were strange. It wasn't that they were terribly painful. They were nothing more than occasional twinges, but the twinges always occurred in the same spot, just over her right eye. And the fact that she was getting *any* kind of headache was especially weird. With her genetic makeup, Amy was physically perfect and never got sick.

Her thoughts must have made her frown, because her mother asked, "Is something wrong?" She looked suddenly concerned, which wasn't unusual. Nancy had always been a worrier where Amy was concerned. Over the past year, she'd become a little looser in her restrictions and warnings and general nagging, but she was still very motherly.

"I'm fine," Amy said brightly. There was no way she was going to tell her mother about the headaches.

Nancy would only make Amy see Dr. Dave Hopkins for an exam, and she would probably cancel her conference. There was no way Amy would give up a weekend of freedom. She was looking forward to a little vacation from her mother's constant concern. Not to mention late nights, junk food, and all the TV she wanted.

two

Monica arrived at the Candler home early Friday morning. She wasn't alone.

"This is Sunshine," she announced, introducing the thin-faced college girl at her side. "I've been giving Sunshine art lessons, and she pays me by running errands and doing odd jobs."

Amy had never met anyone named Sunshine before, and the name didn't suit this girl at all. Her complexion was sallow, her mouth was downturned, and her eyebrows were at an angle that made her look permanently unhappy. At the moment, the girl's arms were full of

Monica's latest project—an enormous wall hanging, embroidered and appliquéd and studded with sequins. The artistic endeavor suited Monica, who favored flamboyant clothes and always had brightly colored hair—kelly green this month. Sunshine, on the other hand, was wearing a gray sacklike dress, and carrying the bright hanging only made her look even more washed-out.

Nancy Candler wasn't disturbed by Monica's companion. She was used to the unusual friends Monica brought around. Besides, she was too frantic to give Sunshine more than a passing glance.

"Hello, Sunshine, nice to meet you. Where *is* that taxi?"

Amy and Monica stepped outside to look. A car with a driver was idling across the street, but it was just an ordinary green car, not a taxi. At the same moment, the door to the Morgan house next door opened, and Tasha came out. She was looking pretty glum.

"They're going to make me take skiing lessons," she announced mournfully.

"Well, look on the bright side," Amy said.

"What's the bright side?"

"After a day of skiing, you hang around the lodge in front of a blazing fire and drink hot chocolate."

That didn't impress Tasha. "Yeah, great, but you have

to get through the day of skiing first." Her parents were coming out now, laden with bags.

"Where's Eric?" Monica asked.

Tasha's scowl deepened. "The lucky creep. He broke his arm playing basketball yesterday so he doesn't have to go."

Amy didn't think a broken arm sounded like great luck, and she asked Mrs. Morgan how Eric was doing.

"Oh, he'll be fine," Mrs. Morgan assured Amy. "Of course, he's terribly disappointed to miss this trip. Monica, could you check in on him this weekend? I've left plenty of food."

"Sure, no problem," Monica said.

"And Amy, maybe you could drop by if you have a minute. I know Eric would like some company."

Amy doubted that *she* was the kind of company Eric wanted, but she agreed to visit. As the Morgans piled into their car, the taxi for Nancy finally arrived.

"Mom!" Amy yelled.

Her mother hurried out with her suitcase. "Sweetie, be good and don't get into any trouble," she said to Amy. When she leaned closer to give her a kiss, she whispered, "And keep an eye on that Sunshine girl, okay? She seems a little strange."

The taxi driver was honking impatiently now, and

there was no time for Nancy to say more. Amy and Monica waved as the car pulled away.

That was when Amy felt her first twinge of the day. It was faint, not sharp, but it was definitely there. She put a hand to her head.

A soft voice behind her made her jump. "Do you have a headache?"

Amy whirled around. Sunshine stood there, gazing at her solemnly.

"Oh no, it's nothing," Amy said quickly. "I was just thinking."

"Thinking," Sunshine repeated. "That's good. As long as you're thinking about today, about the here and now. Not yesterday. Not tomorrow. Be in the moment. Be Zen."

"Yes." Amy didn't know what else to say. There was definitely something strange about the way the girl was staring at her.

Monica didn't seem to notice. "Sunshine, come help me unpack."

Obediently, Sunshine followed Monica back into the house. Amy didn't particularly want to join them, so she decided to go see Eric.

The Morgans' door was unlocked, and she let herself in. She found Eric upstairs in his room, sprawled on his bed, with a set of headphones covering his ears. The music must have been loud because he didn't hear Amy coming up the stairs, and he let out an involuntary shriek when he saw her at the door.

She grinned and he frowned. With his good arm, he pulled off the headset. "You should have knocked," he informed her.

"You wouldn't have heard me," she replied. "How's your arm?"

"How does it look?" he responded gruffly.

She eyed the white cast and sling with sympathy. "Broken. Does it hurt?"

"Nah," he said. But the strain in his eyes told her otherwise. That was why he was acting so coldly, too. He didn't want her to see that he was in pain. Even before he became Mister Cool, Eric had had a tendency to do the macho thing.

Then she recalled the time when they'd been at Wilderness Adventure together and Eric had sprained his ankle. Amy had carried him on her back out of the woods. By then, he'd accepted that Amy would always be smarter and stronger than he was, and he'd still adored her. The memory brought a pang to her heart.

She sat down on the edge of his bed and considered her next words carefully. He wouldn't want her pity, but she wanted him to know she cared. She let him have her true opinion of his situation.

"This stinks."

He could accept that. "No kidding."

"I'll bet you hate to miss the skiing."

"It's a lot worse than that," he said. "I'm off the basketball team for the rest of the season."

"Well, the season's almost over, isn't it?" she asked reasonably.

It wasn't the right thing to say. He scowled. "That's not the point." Clearly, he wanted *some* sympathy.

The phone by his bed rang, and he picked it up. "Yeah? Hi. Yeah, it's broken. I'm out of commission. You going away this weekend? Oh. Rafting, huh? Cool."

While Eric talked to his friend, Amy looked around the room. It hadn't changed much since the last time she had been up there. Same kickboxing poster, same blown-up photo of Michael Jordan. No pictures of *her*, of course, but there never had been any. Eric wasn't the romantic type.

Still, Amy reminded herself again that she couldn't blame the end of their relationship completely on him. There was Andy. . . .

Eric hung up the phone and sighed heavily. "My whole gang's out of town. What am I going to do all weekend?"

"There's a *Real World* marathon on MTV," Amy suggested.

Eric made a gagging sound. He probably thought

watching *The Real World* was beneath the dignity of a high school student.

She noticed a familiar-looking CD package on his desk. "You play Darklands?"

"I'm on level three," Eric told her.

"Is that the garden?"

"Nah, that's level two. I've been out of there for ages."

"Chris is stuck in the garden."

Eric snorted. "Figures."

She had to bite her tongue to keep from snapping at him. Since the first time Eric had seen Chris, with his sullen expression and his black leather jacket, he had been convinced that Chris was some kind of hoodlum-gangster-juvenile delinquent. He wouldn't even try to get to know Amy's friend.

Mentally, she counted to ten and recalled her mother's words when Amy had complained to her about Eric's attitude. "He's going through a phase," Nancy had told her. "Give him time. He'll come out of it."

She decided to appeal to Eric's ego. "Maybe you could help Chris. You don't have to hang out with him," she added hastily, knowing that the mere thought of Eric's befriending Chris was out of the question. "But isn't there a way you can network computers and play online? It would give you something to do this weekend while all your buds are away."

Eric was noncommittal. "Maybe."

"I'll leave you his e-mail address," she said, and scrawled it on the pad on his desk. "And I'll give him yours. Okay?"

"Whatever." Eric picked up the remote control, aimed it at the TV, and clicked. A basketball game appeared, and Amy knew she wouldn't be getting any more of his attention.

"See you," she said, starting toward the door.

"Hey, Amy?"

"What?"

"Um . . . thanks for coming by."

She smiled. It was good to get even a tiny glimpse of the nice guy she knew was still there, buried under Eric's cool façade.

"I'll stop by tomorrow," she promised.

Outside, she noticed that the green car was still idling across the street, and the driver was still behind the wheel. She'd heard about thieves who watched for people to go out of town so they could rob their homes. She tried to get a good look at the driver, but sunglasses covered the top half of his face, and the bottom half was hidden by a beard. Suddenly, she felt that strange twinge again.

Amy shook her head, as if she could shake out the sensation, but it didn't go away. Feeling uneasy, she wondered what could be causing the twinges and why the bearded man in the green car was now looking at her.

Then the twinge was gone. And when she looked back at the car, she saw that the driver wasn't looking at her anymore. Maybe he never had looked. Maybe she was just being paranoid.

But the uneasiness persisted, even as Amy went into her own house. Monica was in the dining room. She'd spread her wall hanging out on the table. Amy joined her.

"It's pretty," she said.

"Thanks. It still needs a lot of work. Maybe a lace inset in this corner. Or some fringe down here. Sunshine?" she shouted toward the stairs. "Do you know where I left my box of thread?"

Amy left Monica to contemplate her masterpiece and started up the stairs to her room. She met Sunshine, who was on her way down.

"Monica's looking for her box of thread," Amy told the young woman. As she spoke, she realized she was getting another twinge in her head. Or was she just feeling uncomfortable because of the way Sunshine was staring at her?

Hurrying past Sunshine, Amy went into her room and shut the door firmly behind her. But even in the safety and familiarity of her own room, she couldn't shake off the uneasiness. She went to the window and looked out. The green car was still outside. Then something in the room caught her eye.

Her computer screen was lit up. She'd written some e-mails that morning, but she was absolutely sure she'd shut down the computer. She went over to look at it.

A screen saver—a swirl of bright colors that roamed the screen in random patterns—was flashing back and forth and up and down. Her usual screen saver displayed flying toasters. Where had this psychedelic pattern come from?

And another thing . . . why was her bottom dresser drawer open? It was the drawer where she kept out-of-season clothes, and she was absolutely sure she hadn't opened it lately. Someone had been in her room.

Amy ran back downstairs. Sunshine was now sitting at the dining room table cutting lengths of thread. Her expressionless eyes moved to Amy's face, and the word *zombie* crept into Amy's head.

She heard water running in the kitchen and found Monica there, filling a kettle. "Hi, want some tea?"

"No thanks. Monica . . . were you in my bedroom?"

"No, why?" Monica turned to her. "Is something missing?"

"No. . . . It just feels like someone was poking around."

Monica wasn't alarmed. "It might have been Sunshine. She was exploring the house. She likes to sense the vibrations and feel the presence of spirits."

"There are no spirits in this house," Amy said sharply.

"Yeah, that's what she said. I'm sure she didn't take anything, though. She's not a thief."

No, not a thief, Amy thought. But what? She left the kitchen and passed through the dining room, aware of Sunshine's spooky eyes on her. What was Sunshine really doing here? Why did Amy think it had something to do with *her*? And that man in the green car *had* been looking at her. The more she thought about it, the more sure she was. And what were these stupid twinges in her head? Was she imagining all this? Was she losing her mind?

She suddenly wished her mother was home. Nancy always listened to Amy and knew how to make her feel better. But Nancy wasn't there, and as much as Amy liked Monica, she didn't want to hear her neighbor talk about the mystical significance of feelings.

So Amy did the only thing she could think of to cheer herself up. Armed with potato chips, assorted dips, sodas, and a bag of cookies, she barricaded herself in her room, turned on the MTV *Real World* marathon, and tried to get caught up in the lives of twenty-somethings who had nothing to do but fall in and out of love with each other.

The twinges persisted all day long—even after Sunshine left and the green car across the street was gone. Well into the evening, lying in bed, Amy experienced the uneasiness, the feeling of being watched, the sensation of somehow being in danger—but from what, or whom? She was safe and sound in her own home. Monica was downstairs watching TV. Amy had closed her windows and taken the extra precaution of pulling the latch that locked them from the inside. Still, she had trouble falling asleep.

Only, she *must* have fallen asleep at some point—because she was woken up by a sound. A tapping sound.

In the darkness, with her eyes open, she tried to identify the source of the sound. It wasn't coming from the door. It wasn't a mouse scurrying inside one of the walls. The tapping was coming from her window.

Her heart thumping, Amy sat up.

Don't be scared, she told herself. If there's someone out there trying to get in, you're probably stronger and smarter than he or she is. You've taken on people twice your size and beaten them. You've used your wits to escape countless times.

Creeping out of bed, Amy padded silently to the window. *Why* had she let her mother buy such thick, opaque drapes? Even with her keen vision, Amy couldn't see through them.

Slowly, carefully, holding her breath, she touched the opening of the drapes with her fingertips and brushed them aside just a crack. She jumped back as a bunch of little pebbles hit the glass. That was what was causing the tapping. Someone was throwing pebbles at her window. Sunshine? The man in the green car? Some enemy she didn't even know she had?

None of the above. Even though the figure wasn't illuminated, she had no trouble making him out. Her breath came out in a rush. There would be no one to beat up tonight, no one to escape from.

Quickly, she unhooked the latch, opened the window, and leaned out. She spoke in a whisper because she didn't want to wake Monica, but she knew the person standing below would have no problem hearing her. His ears were as sensitive to sound as hers were.

"Andy!"

three

Night shadows obscured his expression, but Amy could feel his tension from the stiff way he stood beneath her window. She motioned in the direction of the back door and then ran downstairs to open it.

Andy slipped inside, and Amy caught her breath. He looked awful. He was still blond and handsome, of course, but his hair was matted and dirty, his shirt was torn, and there were fresh bruises on his face.

"Is your mother up?" he whispered.

"She's out of town. Monica is sleeping on the living room sofa." With a finger to her lips, she led him down the hall, past the living room, and upstairs. There were snacks in her bedroom left over from her afternoon eating binge, and Andy eyed them hungrily.

"Eat," she told him, and he did, wolfing down potato chips and chugging an entire can of soda. Between bites and gulps, he muttered something about not having eaten in thirty-six hours. She watched him silently, trying to collect her feelings.

Andy Denker . . . the male version of herself. One of twelve genetically engineered clones conceived two years before the Amys. He lived in San Francisco, and he drifted in and out of her life at odd moments. Their paths had first crossed in the wilds of the Northwest, then at a café in Paris, and most recently, on a remote tropical island. This was the first time they'd been face to face in Los Angeles.

"What are you doing here?" Amy finally asked him.

"Looking for you," he said. "I walked and hitchhiked from San Francisco."

She was flattered. "Gee, you must have really missed me."

"No. I came here to warn you."

Her smile faded. "About what?"

Andy went to her window and looked out. "I can't stay long," he said. "They'll come looking for me here."

"They?"

"The organization. We're in danger, Amy. All of us. Well, at least the ones who got off the island."

This wasn't really news to her. The organization had been in the background for a long time. They'd never given up on the plan to get all the clones together, to indoctrinate them and push them toward the destiny for which they'd been created—the evolution of an entire race of superior beings. She'd had her share of encounters with the organization, and so had Andy. But she'd never seen him look this unnerved by it all.

"What happened?" she asked.

"We're being monitored," he told her. "Not just where we are, but what we're thinking and planning. Amy . . . have you been getting headaches?"

"Sort of," she admitted. "Just little twinges now and then."

He nodded grimly. "So have I. I've been in contact with two other Andys, and they're getting the headaches too. And I think I know why."

His theory was simple—and overwhelming. "Back at the island, electrodes were attached to our heads. They were supposed to reprogram our genes or something, remember?"

Amy remembered. Some of the clones had been able

to harness the emotional strength to fight the procedure. But according to Andy, the organization had succeeded in another goal.

"They implanted something, either a computer chip or some sort of tracing device. I'm not sure which, but the organization has some kind of control over us now. They're messing with our heads, reading our minds. Maybe they're even thinking for us!"

Andy was truly frightened. Amy could hear it in his voice. She tried to speak soothingly. "Andy, calm down. You're safe for the time being. Why don't you get some sleep, and—"

He interrupted her. "There's no time for sleep! They're everywhere, Amy! They're all around us, inside and outside. Don't you feel it? Can't you tell that they're closing in on you?"

A vision of Sunshine and the man in the green car passed through her mind. She eyed him doubtfully. "I'm not sure. . . ."

"And you can't trust anyone," he added bitterly. "Want to know how I figured it all out?"

She nodded.

"My so-called father. He's one of them."

Amy drew in her breath. "Andy, no!"

"We went camping together, and he was talking in

his sleep one night. He kept mumbling some letters and numbers, and I couldn't get them out of my head. It sounded like a password, so I used it to access his e-mail on his computer."

Amy felt sick. "What did you find?"

"Notes about me, sent to someone called the Director. This Director referred to my dear old dad as the Caretaker." He fell silent.

"And?" Amy prompted him.

"It was about the headaches, how he shouldn't be alarmed if I complain about them. That the implant was for our own good. That's as far as I got before I heard him coming. I took off that night."

"Ohmigod," Amy murmured. "Your own father."

"Who isn't really my father, as you know. Just like your mother isn't your mother."

Amy looked at him sharply. "Andy, don't you dare even suggest for one second that my mother is involved with the organization."

He shrugged and pushed a lock of hair out of his eyes. "Look, all I know is that the jerk I've been calling Dad for sixteen years is ready to throw me to the lions. And I'm not going to make it easy for him—or them."

She'd never heard him talk like this before—so aggressive, so hostile. For a brief moment, Amy wondered if this was really *her* Andy or one of the other clones posing as him. But then he reached out and clutched her hand. "Come with me," he said.

That was when she felt the magnetic power, the attraction she had only ever felt for him. It was a weird sensation, and she didn't know how to describe it. It wasn't even a boyfriend thing. It was something stronger, a sense of being connected in a way that was both remote and intense at the same time.

"Where are you going?" she wanted to know.

"I'm not sure. I've got an idea, but I don't know if it will work." His head jerked up. "Did you hear that?"

She had. It was the sound of someone climbing the stairs. She motioned for him to stay away from the bedroom door and opened it a crack. "Monica?"

The figure on the stairs rubbed her eyes. "I thought I heard voices."

"I was watching TV," Amy told her.

"Oh. It's after midnight. You should get to sleep."

"I will," Amy promised her, and closed the door. When she turned back to Andy, he was looking out her window.

"Isn't that what's-his-name, the guy who was at Wilderness Adventure? Eric? What's the matter with his arm?"

Amy joined him at the window. Sure enough, Eric was visible, sitting at his desk, looking at a computer screen. "He broke it," Amy said. "I'll bet it's keeping him from sleeping. His family went skiing for the weekend, and he's all alone."

"He knows about us, doesn't he? You trust him."

"Absolutely," Amy said.

"You think he'd let me stay over?"

Amy didn't know what to say. It was true that Eric knew about Andy, and he didn't like the guy. As to whether Eric would be able to rise above the bad feelings to help him, Amy couldn't say. There was only one way to find out.

Fortunately, Monica had fallen back into a deep sleep and they slipped by her and out the front door with no trouble. And fortunately again, Eric had carelessly forgotten to lock the Morgans' front door. She'd have to say something to him about that.

At least this time he didn't have his headset on, and he heard them come into the house. He met them at the top of the stairs with a baseball bat. When he saw who it was, he lowered the bat, but the expression he gave them wasn't exactly welcoming.

"What's *he* doing here?" Eric asked with a nod toward Andy.

"He needs a place to stay," Amy told him.

"Just for the night," Andy added. "I'll be gone in the morning."

Eric looked back and forth between the two of them, and Amy realized she was wearing the not-too-long T-shirt she'd been sleeping in. Flushing, she tried to pull it down. Andy, meanwhile, was giving Eric the same story he'd told Amy. While he talked, she looked at Eric's computer screen to see what he'd been doing.

There was an instant message conversation going on, and she was pleased to see Chris's screen name, CS87.

If u wanna net, ok. Are u there?

She typed a response. **Hi, it's me, Amy.**

She waited for the next line.

What r u doing there?

She answered: **A friend needs place 2 stay. I brought him here.**

What friend? he asked.

She wrote: **Long story, tell u 2morrow.**

"It's okay," Andy said. "Eric's going to let me stay."

"You gotta be out of here before my folks get back," Eric warned him.

"I will."

"Thanks, Eric," Amy said warmly.

Meanwhile, Andy had collapsed on the closest bed. "Hey, not there," Eric said. "You can sleep in my sister's room."

"I'll be back first thing in the morning," Amy prom-ised, and left them to sort out their sleeping arrange-

36

ments. Even with her worry for Andy, she couldn't help feeling a little warm and fuzzy. This couldn't be easy for Eric, but his inner good guy was coming through. And now he was about to start networking with Chris, too! All the boys in her life were coming together. It was weird . . . but kind of nice.

four

When Amy woke up the next morning, the first thing she did was go to the window and try to see into Eric's room. But the blinds were drawn, so she dressed rapidly to go over there.

Downstairs, Monica was struggling to put the sofa bed back in the sofa position, and Amy paused to give her a hand. As she did, she heard sounds in the kitchen. "Is someone here?"

"Sunshine," Monica replied happily. "She makes my breakfast every morning. She says poor nutrition can block creative energy. She's very in touch with the inner self, you know."

Whose inner self? Amy wondered. The strange young woman appeared just then. "Breakfast is ready," Sunshine told them. "Whole-wheat buttermilk pancakes with blueberries."

"Sounds yummy," Monica said. "C'mon, Amy, let's pig out."

"No thanks, I'm not hungry," Amy replied.

Sunshine turned her gloomy eyes on Amy. "You should eat breakfast. I sense a nutritional imbalance in your aura."

"I can live with it," Amy said. "I gotta be somewhere." As she left her house, her suspicions kicked into high gear. Why was Sunshine so concerned with her well-being? Was it possible that she'd taken this job with Monica just to get closer to *her*? She had to get Andy's opinion about this.

Eric had finally remembered to lock the front door, so she had to knock. He must have already been downstairs because he answered right away.

But Andy's opinion of Sunshine wouldn't be forthcoming anytime soon.

"He's not here," Eric told her.

"What do you mean, he's not here?"

"Just what I said," Eric said irritably. "When I woke up this morning, he was gone."

"Gone where?"

"How should *I* know? He's your friend, not mine."

Amy paced the living room. "Eric, why did you let him leave?"

"Hey, I was sleeping!"

"You should have kept an eye on him!" she scolded. "He told you he's in danger."

"Well, no one came to get him," Eric informed her. "I locked the door before I went to sleep, and it was still locked this morning."

Amy stared at him. "What about the back door?"

"That's always locked," Eric told her, but Amy went to check anyway. He was right. Like the front door, it was locked from the inside, and the chain was on the latch.

"How did Andy get out?" she wondered aloud.

Eric shrugged. "Maybe he jumped out a window." But all the windows in the house were shut tight. "Or maybe he's developed even more powers than you've got," Eric volunteered. "You were always so impressed with him. Maybe he can walk through walls now."

Amy didn't dignify that with a response. All she gave Eric was one withering look before walking out the door. But once outside, she didn't know where to go or how to start looking for Andy. If he was hitchhiking, he could be miles away, and she didn't know what direction he'd head in. And how *had* he left Eric's place?

Walking aimlessly, Amy tried to think about logical answers. She was so caught up in trying to work out things out that she almost missed the green car.

It was in the same place it had been yesterday, and the bearded man was behind the wheel. As she stared at the car, its motor started up. The driver began easing it out of its space.

Panic filled her. For once, Amy didn't care if any neighbors happened to be looking out their windows. She took off at top speed, leaping over a fence to get away from the road. If that man was after her, he would have to chase her on foot—and if he wasn't a champion runner or a genetically engineered clone, he'd never catch up to her. She ran through backyards, trying to hold on to a sense of direction so she could get herself to a safe place.

She ended up in front of the Martins' front door. Be home, please be home, she prayed. Her prayer was answered.

"Hi, Amy," Mrs. Martin said warmly. "C'mon in. Chris is in his room on his computer." She laughed lightly. "I'm not sure it was such a good idea, getting him that computer. We never see him anymore!"

Amy tried to respond with a light laugh, but it came out sounding more like a high-pitched squeal. Mrs. Martin didn't seem to notice that she was on the edge of hysteria, and she didn't question the way Amy flew up the stairs.

Chris knew something was wrong, though. The second Amy burst through his door, his eyebrows shot up and he rose from his seat. "What's the matter?"

"It's Andy. He's disappeared," Amy said breathlessly. "I think he's been abducted. And I think they're after me too."

"Whoa! Wait a minute," Chris said. "Calm down and start from the beginning. Who's Andy? And who's *they*?"

Amy first went to his window. The leafy branches of a tree partially obscured her view, but there didn't seem to be anyone lurking out in the street. With a sigh, she sank down on his bed.

"Andy's the friend I mentioned on the instant message last night. He's . . . he's like me. Only a guy. And he says the organization planted something in our heads. That they're following us or reading our minds or something bad like that. Now they've got him. Which means I've got to hide. But if they can read my mind, then there's nowhere safe! Sunshine watches me when I'm inside, the man in the green car when I'm outside, and I don't know where Andy went, and—and—I don't know where to go!"

She paused to catch her breath and realized that Chris was completely bewildered. She hadn't been making any sense at all.

But at least he didn't mock her the way Eric had. "Wait a second," he said, and tapped a few keys on his computer.

"What are you doing?" she asked.

"Telling Eric I gotta go for now."

Despite her distress, Amy was curious. "Are you going to play Darklands with him?"

"I'm not sure. Maybe. We're going to try to set up a network between our computers so we can compete inside the same game. It's weird, though, because I can tell he doesn't really want me to have access. Your friend Eric doesn't trust me."

"He's not my friend," Amy said curtly. "He didn't watch out for Andy and he doesn't even care that we're in trouble." She was feeling calmer now and began explaining again.

Chris already knew a lot of her story. She'd told him about Project Crescent and why the scientists had abandoned it. He knew about the organization and what they wanted. Now she explained about Andy and their history. When she described their experiences together in Paris, though, she caught a glimmer of jealousy in Chris's eyes.

"It sounds like you two have something special going," he said gruffly.

Amy sighed. "We have a relationship," she admitted. "But I don't know what it means. Sometimes I think Andy is more like a brother than anything else. What I do know is that he and I are in the same situation. The same danger. This—this bonds us. Do you understand?"

"I guess."

She had to accept that as the best Chris could do. She went on to tell him about the island and Andy's theory about the implant in their heads. She told him about Sunshine and the bearded man in the green car.

"Are you sure they're part of this?" he asked. "Maybe that chip is making you feel paranoid."

"I don't know," Amy replied honestly. "I haven't the slightest idea what it's doing to me. All I know is, I need to find a safe place to hide for a while. That's the only way I stand a chance of figuring out how to disable this thing in my head."

"You could stay here," Chris said.

Amy shook her head. "Thanks, but the organization could trace me here as well as in my own home."

"Then they can trace you anywhere," Chris said. "There's no safe place, Amy. Not on earth."

Chris was right. There was nowhere to run. If the organization could access her mind, they could access her body. They would find her no matter what.

"What am I going to do?" she asked Chris helplessly, knowing full well he couldn't help her.

Chris was deep in thought. "Tell me again what they tried to do to you on the island. That business with the electrodes."

"It had to do with shifting the DNA code in a genome remnant," she said. "They believe that if we don't possess a conscience, we won't care about anyone or anything. Except personal survival."

"And you fought it off?"

She nodded. "I concentrated on remembering the most emotional moments of my life."

"Your brain has to be incredibly powerful," Chris noted. "It's like your thoughts were pure energy."

"I don't know how it worked," she replied. "All I know is that I wasn't affected. Neither was Andy. But some other clones were changed. I guess they didn't fight the procedure."

Chris considered this. "I don't know anything about brain waves," he confessed. "But it seems to me, if you had the energy to battle something like that, maybe you've got the energy to . . ." He hesitated.

"To what?" she prompted him.

"This is going to sound crazy," he admitted. "But maybe your mind can take you someplace. Someplace not on earth."

Amy was taken aback. "You mean, use my brain-power to build a spaceship and go to Mars?" She meant that as a joke, but then she wondered if that was along the lines of what Chris was thinking. "Or maybe I should just get myself to Cape Canaveral and hitch a ride on the next shuttle NASA sends off." She shuddered. It was not a pleasant image.

Chris shook his head. "I was thinking about Darklands."

"Darklands?" Amy looked at him in disbelief. "Darklands is a *game*, Chris. Not a real place."

"But maybe you could go *into* the game. No one would ever find you there. Like you said, it's not a real place."

"You're not making sense," Amy said. "If it's not a real place, how can I exist in it?"

"Maybe your body can't," he replied. "But it's your mind we have to worry about, right? That's how the organization is connected to you. If your consciousness was in Darklands . . ."

"Where would my body be?" she asked.

"I don't know," Chris replied honestly.

Amy got up and paced the room. "This is insane.

What you're talking about is science-fiction stuff. It's like that movie with the shape-shifters, who could morph into a table or a chair."

"It's all molecules," Chris said. "Just in different forms."

Amy rolled her eyes. "I think it's a little more complicated than that."

"Look, all I know is that you can do things with your head that other people can't do," Chris said. "Remember when you were struck by lightning and started reading everyone's minds? Lightning doesn't have that effect on everyone. So maybe you have the ability to get yourself into this game."

"How?"

"Same way you fought off those electric impulses. Concentration. Put all your energy into getting there."

Amy went to the computer and looked at the screen. Chris was still stuck in the garden level. At least it didn't look like a bad place to hang out.

"I'd be in control," he said. "I'd zap the Intruders, and if you got into any trouble, I could click on you and move you somewhere." He hesitated. "Unless you're like your friend Eric—and you feel you can't trust me."

"Eric's not my friend," Amy replied automatically. "And I do trust you." She sat down at the computer. "What should I do?"

Chris had paused the program. Now he hit something, and the image came to life—birds flew across the sky, and Amy could hear wind and water splashing in the fountain.

"Concentrate," Chris said. "Visualize. See yourself inside the garden."

Obediently, Amy closed her eyes and pictured herself sitting under a tree. When she opened her eyes, she was still looking at the screen.

"It's not working," she declared.

"Is this how you fought off those electric impulses?" Chris shook his head. "You're not really trying, Amy. Think about the organization. Think about what they want to do with you and Andy and all those other clones. They're coming after you. They're getting closer! You have to get away, you have to hide!"

The urgency in his voice gripped her. The panic she'd been feeling earlier began to rise up in her again. If she could channel this fear . . . What they would do to her . . . the experiments, the probing, the imprisonment . . . the world changing . . . the power of nature destroyed, the human race no longer subject to natural evolution . . . world domination by a genetically superior, unfeeling species . . . The horror of it all was overwhelming. She had to stop this. She couldn't let them get her! She had to hide!

She could feel the pressure, the internal noise she'd experienced back on the island, penetrating every cell of her body. Her body was in limbo—moving and still at the same time. Darkness, impenetrable darkness surrounded her. Then nothingness. She was spinning into a void.

And then—sunshine. The sound of birds, the smell of roses. Hearing, seeing, feeling . . . being. Under a tree in a beautiful garden.

f5ye

unny how the game was called Darklands when it was actually very light and bright inside this world. Almost too light and bright. It seemed to take a few minutes for Amy's eyes to adjust. Or was it a few seconds? Time was irrelevant here.

Amy realized that her eyesight wasn't going to improve. It was as if she was looking through a fine haze. She could make out everything she'd seen on the screen—the fountain, the statues, the castle turrets off in the distance. But it all had an artificial look to it.

Which made perfectly good sense, she reminded herself. This was an artificial place. The rosebushes over there smelled more like rose-scented perfume than actual flowers. And the statues of the angel and the unicorn would never be so white in a public garden.

On closer inspection, Amy saw that the roses actually had unnaturally even blossoms and that they were all the same size. The statues seemed to be made of synthetic material. Well, why not? This wasn't the real world, after all.

Enough thinking about her environment. What about her? Was she real? Was her body here, as well as her mind? She held a hand in front of her face, and though she could see it, it didn't seem any more real than anything else around her. Exasperated, Amy stopped pondering what she was or how she existed in Darklands. This whole experience went contrary to the laws of nature, and she decided she was better off not understanding any of it.

She felt a gentle push. Automatically, she began to move in the direction of the fountain. It was Chris, of course—he was moving her. She wondered if he was in total control or whether she'd be able to stand still if she wanted to. She tried stopping and felt a tugging, but it was easy to resist. She grinned.

Okay, Chris, I'll trust you, but you can't push me around!
Had she actually said that, or was she just thinking

it? Could Chris hear her? She could almost see him, rolling his eyes and grimacing in exasperation at the screen. How did she appear to him there? Probably a plastic version of herself. Like a doll.

There was another tug, and she thought she knew what Chris wanted. He was trying to get her to search for clues, a passage to the castle, something that would help him get to the next level. Well, there was plenty of time for that. Now that she knew Chris couldn't completely control her, she wanted to explore at her own pace. Right now, she just wanted to appreciate the feeling of being safe.

But she wasn't safe, of course. A vaguely familiar, spooky sound seemed to be coming from behind her. It was a low whistling. She turned.

The Intruder looked a lot scarier from inside the game. The hooded skull bore a hideous insane smile, and the thing was coming right at her. Immediately, Amy went into a fighting stance, one foot in front of the other, arms raised karate style. This was exciting. What would the creature feel like? How much strength would it have?

She would not find out. Before the thing was even within striking distance, it froze, let out an unearthly shriek, and exploded. Obviously, Chris had zapped it.

Amy was disappointed. *Hey, Chris, give me a crack at it*

53

before you blow it away, okay? She looked around to see if another one was going to pop up right away. Then she realized that Chris couldn't control the appearance of the Intruders, which had been programmed by the game's creators. Chris could only destroy them after they appeared. She'd have to keep her eyes and ears open. It would be cool to take one on and destroy it before Chris could obliterate it electronically.

She continued strolling. She moved around the flowers and the statues, but there was nothing very interesting behind them—just more flowers, clusters of rocks, a bench. She went to the fountain and peered in. She saw coins at the bottom—not real coins, of course, just flat disks that could pass as pennies from a distance.

Except for one of them. Bending over, she could see that a particular coin, the same shape and size as the others, bore some markings. She reached for it, but her arm wasn't long enough. She'd have to go into the fountain.

The water was clear, and the temperature was moderate—perfect, like everything else. She picked up the interesting coin from the bottom and climbed out.

The number 749 was engraved on the coin. This had to be a clue to something. She wondered if Chris could see the coin and numbers too. Were they the key to another level? Would the coin help her get across the moat? Since she was stuck here, she might as well help Chris get to level three.

Moving in the direction of the castle, Amy realized she wasn't wet from her plunge in the fountain. In a way, that didn't surprise her—it was just another indication of her unnatural environment. When she reached the moat, she looked around for a way to use the coin to get her across the murky water.

She supposed she could jump in and swim to the castle, but the water looked really nasty. There had to be another way. Maybe a canoe was hidden in the tall weeds that grew along the banks of the moat.

Amy moved along the water's edge, not knowing how much time had passed. All she knew was that she had found nothing that indicated a way across the moat. She couldn't find anyplace to use the numbers or the coin.

C'mon, Chris, help me out. This is getting boring.

As Amy kicked a stone out of her way, something caught her eye. It was a flicker of silver. Amy began pushing away more stones and then clapped her hands in delight. Under the mound of rocks was a large, flat metal plate with a handle. So she'd been right. The angel pointed to the mound of stones in order to get the player to click on them. If only Chris had listened.

Amy pulled at the handle and lifted the plate off the

ground. It had been covering a flight of stairs leading down into the ground. That was the route—you crossed the moat by means of a tunnel.

The stairs were steep, more like a ladder, and without anything like a rail to hold on to. So Amy moved slowly to keep her balance. She didn't know what would happen if she fell, and she didn't want to find out. She wasn't really scared because she knew Chris could click her out of a serious problem. But she didn't particularly want any unpleasant sensations, and the image of that nasty, murky water was still in her head.

Still, climbing down was taking forever. Surely, Chris should be able to move her to the bottom with a click much faster than she could reach it on her own. But he was making her experience the entire boring descent one step at a time. Was this his way of punishing her for taking off on her own?

Very funny, Chris, ha ha. She'd never been crazy about narrow, enclosed spaces. Finally, she made out a dim light. It gave her something to aim for. It wasn't much longer before she found herself at the bottom of the ladder.

The tunnel itself was creepy too. At regular intervals, candles flickered in sconces on the walls, throwing ghostly shadows on the path. Amy tried not to think about being underground and moved as quickly as she could. She kept looking for a light marking the end of the tunnel, but the tunnel seemed endless.

Then she heard the whistle. It was fainter than the last time, but the eerie hiss warned her that an Intruder was fast approaching. She wouldn't mind if Chris zapped this one immediately. The notion of fighting in the tunnel wasn't appealing.

But the whistle continued, and it was getting louder. Amy started running. If she could avoid being overtaken by the Intruder until she was out of the tunnel, they could have a fair fight. But down here, there wasn't enough space to move around.

The whistle was shrill. *Okay, Chris, zap it. Now!*

But Chris wasn't doing anything to help her out. When a flickering candle gave her a glimpse of a ladder up ahead, she sprinted for it, and as she approached, she leaped to the highest rung she could reach. She was climbing steadily, but the whistle wasn't fading. She sensed that the Intruder was just below her on the ladder. At last, she could make out a light above her—the exit, she presumed—and that gave her the encouragement to climb even faster.

But not fast enough. It was a shock when she felt a hand grip her ankle. It was even more of a shock when she realized she couldn't pull free.

six

idn't she have her super-strength here in Darklands? Or were these Intruders supernaturally strong? Amy tugged, trying to pull away, but the Intruder held tight.

Okay, Chris, this isn't funny! Zap it!

Then she realized why Chris wasn't doing anything.

Amy, it's me!

She wasn't sure if she actually heard the voice or just felt it. How did the senses operate in here, anyway? It didn't matter—she knew the voice.

Andy!

I'm right behind you. Just don't close the lid on me when you get out. Her ankle was released, and she scrambled to the top of the ladder. Once outside, she collapsed on the ground. Seconds later, Andy collapsed next to her.

Hi.

Hi. So this is where you went when you left Eric's.

Yeah. He left the game on when he went to bed. I still don't know how I managed to get myself into it.

It's something to do with energy and molecules. So Eric doesn't know you're here?

I'm not sure. Maybe he's figured it out. If he's playing, he must be able to see me on the screen.

Has he zapped Intruders for you?

I haven't seen any Intruders.

Chris is zapping them for me, so I'm sure he'll zap the ones coming after you too. Are we safe here?

It depends on what you mean by safe.

What do you mean, it depends on what I mean?

I mean, I don't know. Have you had any headaches since you've been inside Darklands?

No.

Neither have I. I'm thinking maybe the chip doesn't work in this place. So the organization can't reach us here.

Amy had more questions, such as how long he thought they would have to stay inside the game and how they would be able to get out. But she didn't ask any of them because she knew he couldn't know anything more than she did. At least she wasn't alone now.

I'm glad you're here.

Me too. Wow, this is weird.

Of course it's weird, Andy. We're inside a game.

I mean, the fact that I'm not soaking wet. I went into that moat to try to swim across. Then I saw the frog.

What frog?

In the moat. I followed it to the tunnel passage. Isn't that how you found it?

No, I got in through a door. This is interesting, she thought. There was more than one way to move through Darklands. *I went into the fountain and when I got out, I wasn't wet. I guess nothing's very real here. What exactly are we trying to do here, anyway? I mean, what's the goal of the game?*

I don't know. I've never played it before.

Oh, great, she thought. She was with the one teenage boy in the entire universe who didn't play Darklands. She looked on the bright side: At least they'd be playing as equals.

It was interesting the way Andy looked like a drawing of himself here in Darklands. But of course, they would both be drawings, since they were characters here, not real people. Had their real bodies been left back in the real world? Or were these their real bodies, transformed into virtual ones?

If she kept thinking like this, she'd get headaches again. Better to just keep moving.

Let's go to the castle.

Andy agreed. He started to get up, and then frowned. **What's that?** He felt along his backside.

It looks like a piece of paper.

Andy peeled off it off. **It must have stuck to me in the moat.** He read it and frowned. **It's a note.**

What does it say?

"You are in your element."

What's that supposed to mean?

Nothing. Probably just a false clue. He crumpled the paper and tossed it.

How do you know it's a false clue? You said you never played Darklands before.

I know how these games work. They feed you a lot of junk to keep you playing so you'll think it's really hard and complicated.

So how are we supposed to know if a clue is real or fake?

We'll just know. Look, Amy, these games are made for ordinary people to struggle over. We've got superior minds. We'll figure it out.

She wished she had his confidence. At the moment,

she was very glad to know that Chris was operating the game. And it *was* just a game, she kept reminding herself. It was all smoke and shadows and things jumping out at you. Like watching a horror movie—you could enjoy being scared because you knew nothing could really hurt you.

She looked around. *Is that the castle?* All she could see was a turret rising from muddy-looking clouds. It wasn't as distinct as it had been from level two.

In fact, nothing was distinct. Everything was darker, tinged with gray. So this was why it was called Darklands. She could barely see anything. But something sparkled on the ground, and she reached for it.

Don't touch that!

Why not?

Because it could be a trick.

Or it could be a clue.

She picked up the cold, shiny object. It was a knife.

Leave it.

The tone of his voice annoyed her, and she stuck the knife in her pocket. She didn't like anyone giving her orders. But when Andy gripped her hand and started walking, she didn't resist.

Distance took on a whole different meaning here, that was for sure. It had seemed like a long way to the castle, but in what felt like seconds, they were at the door. By its side stood an imposing suit of armor, complete with an ax in one of the hands. Above the door was an ornate carving of a horned and winged gargoyle.

That was fast. Chris probably clicked us here.

Who is this Chris?

A friend. A nice guy.

That's not what Eric told me. He said Chris is a gangster.

That's ridiculous. Hey, this door is locked. How do we get in? Wait, I know! The knife! She withdrew it from her pocket and stuck the point into the keyhole. Nothing happened.

I told you that knife was worthless. There's got to be a key.

Andy began poking around the area, looking under a rock, then feeling around the door frame. Meanwhile, Amy looked around to see if there were any windows, but the castle had the appearance of a fortress, with no access. Now Andy was on his hands and knees, trying to pull up a mat that lay on the ground. Out of the corner of her eye, Amy saw something stir.

Andy, move! she screamed.

The ax just missed him. It stuck in the ground beside a stunned Andy, the knight's hand still gripping it. After the momentary shock wore off, Andy charged the metal monster. It wasn't very solid. Pieces of tin fell to the ground. There wasn't anyone inside.

Andy swore. *That thing almost cut my head off!*

Amy had to admit it looked that way. *Chris wouldn't have let that happen,* she assured him.

Why did he let the arm drop in the first place? Just to scare me?

He's just trying to entertain us. You know, to make the game more fun.

Your friend has a weird idea of what's fun.

Oh come on, Andy, lighten up. It's a game. And look over there! There's a key in the knight's helmet.

Andy went to pick it up and let out another curse. *It's hot! I practically burned myself!*

Amy would have guessed it would be hot—the key was fiery red and glowing. As she watched, the redness faded and the key became blue. *I think it's okay now.*

Oh yeah? Then you pick it up!

She did. The key was cool to the touch. She stuck it into the keyhole, and it fit perfectly.

See? Chris is looking out for us.

He's looking out for you. Your gangster friend doesn't know me.

He knows about you.

You told him about us? He knows what we are?

Of course! He's my friend, and I trust him.

Then why is he making this stupid game so hard for us?

Amy was still playing with the key, trying to get it to catch in the lock. *He wants to make it challenging, that's all. So we won't be bored.*

She kept twisting the key. Then she heard the eerie whistling.

What's that? Andy asked.

Grimly, Amy kept working at the key. *An Intruder's coming. Look behind you.*

She had her back to Andy, but he must have done as she told him to, because he gasped.

Amy—

What?

I'm not bored.

seven

Despite the fact that she'd already seen an Intruder, Amy shivered when she looked at the horrific creature. *It's a game, it's a game,* she kept chanting to herself as the Intruder approached.

What do we do?

Chris will zap it before it reaches us.

But Chris didn't zap it. She remembered what Chris had told her: A player had five seconds to explode the Intruder before it obliterated the game. Had it been five seconds since the Intruder appeared on the scene? The chill Amy was feeling grew stronger, colder, as if the Intruder itself was radiating icy waves.

She was beginning to feel real tension. Was Chris not paying attention? Had he left the game running while he went to the bathroom or something? What were she and Andy supposed to do? How did you fight a virtual monster, anyway?

Andy decided to attack. Once the creature was in contact distance, he went into a kickboxing stance and swung one leg out at the Intruder's skull—or whatever lurked behind the cloak. His foot floated right through it, and the skull remained intact. Andy froze. Literally. He wasn't just unable to move because of fright. Amy could actually see icicles forming on his body.

So this was what Chris had meant when he said the Intruder could obliterate you. Andy was no more than an ice sculpture. Amy would be next.

Or maybe not. The Intruder was gone. She hadn't seen it explode, but obviously Chris had returned from wherever he had been and zapped it. Now could he release Andy from the ice?

Apparently not. Nothing was changing. Amy looked around to see if she could spot an antidote that would return Andy to his normal state. The bleak, dusty gray surroundings provided no such possibilities. Leaning against the castle door, Amy tried to summon up the strength to break it down. It wouldn't budge, but in the process of pushing, she felt warmth on the other side of the door. If she could get Andy inside, maybe the icicles that imprisoned his body would melt.

But how to get him inside? There had to be a way. Amy looked around for a clue, but it was getting darker. She hadn't been able to see much before the Intruder appeared, and now she could see even less. Except for the pinpoint of light from a tiny star above her.

No, not a star—the light came from an eye on the gargoyle. It was blinking on and off. Even though she didn't know much about computer games, she knew the blinking meant something. Obviously, Chris needed to click on the eye, and all she could do was wait for him to figure it out.

The gargoyle continued to blink. *C'mon, Chris,* Amy muttered impatiently. Chris didn't do anything. Maybe she could she click on the eye manually? She estimated the height of the gargoyle and knew that even a flying leap wouldn't bring her close to the carving. She'd have to climb somehow.

The castle walls were smooth. There were no ridges or crevices she could use for a foothold. She needed a ladder, a tree, something tall enough that could get her higher up. But there was nothing at all to climb in this level of Darklands.

Then it hit her: the ice statue.

Amy pushed Andy's stiffened body to a position just

under the gargoyle. Resting a foot on one of his slightly bent frozen knees, she hoisted herself up and wrapped a leg around one of his shoulders. Shivering all the while, she pulled the other leg around and stood up on his shoulders. Stretching, she still couldn't reach the gargoyle. She had to step up and balance herself precariously on his head.

Even then, she was a few inches short. Reaching into her pocket, she pulled out the knife. She was able to touch the gargoyle's blinking eye with the tip of her blade. There was a pinging sound, the eye stopped blinking, and the tiny light remained steady.

She waited for something to happen. Maybe the gargoyle would speak. Maybe the castle door would open. Maybe a hundred squirrels would pop out of a turret and dance across the roof.

Then she felt her feet sliding out from under her. Andy's solid-ice head had become slippery. The next thing she knew, her arms were wrapped around Andy's neck. Clearly, Andy was melting.

You're choking me!

Amy released her arms and dropped to the ground. *Sorry. Are you okay?*

Oh yeah, just fine and dandy. That was a real cute trick your friend Chris pulled. Why didn't he zap that thing?

I don't see why you have to blame Chris. How do you know it wasn't Eric's fault?

Eric wouldn't do a thing like that. He wants to help! He left the game running so I could escape into it.

Huh-uh. He left the game running because he forgot to turn it off. Eric doesn't even like you. Hey, are you feeling warm?

No, I'm not feeling warm, I'm still defrosting. But then, **It is getting a little warmer. What's going on?**

She looked up. The gargoyle's eye was still lit up. That had to be the source of the heat. On a hunch, she tried the key again in the lock on the castle door. This time the door opened.

Andy was right behind her, and they entered the castle together. That was when they discovered the source of the heat they were feeling.

A raging fire was burning inside the castle. And as they turned to run back out, the door slammed shut.

e8ght

It was like waiting at the entrance to the pits of hell. They clung together on the small landing and looked down into the flames. Andy spoke first. He spoke almost casually, but it was clearly an effort on his part.

This is a very sophisticated game. I mean, you can actually feel the heat and smell the fire.

Amy could hear the slight tremor in his voice, and she shared his fear. Her limited experience with Darklands had left her with *some* knowledge of how it normally operated.

It's not supposed to be like this, not when you're playing it. You can see what's happening, and you can hear it, but you can't feel or smell anything. We're not just playing the game, Andy. We're inside it. And after a moment, she added, *I'm starting to think it isn't just a game anymore. If you know what I mean.*

She didn't have to elaborate. Andy knew exactly what she meant. **We're on our own.**

Yes.

She didn't know what had happened to Chris. Or to Eric either, if Eric was even playing the game. But somehow, they had lost control or given up. There would be no help coming from either of them. If Amy and Andy were going to win at Darklands, they would have to accomplish it all by themselves.

Win . . . ha. If they were going to *survive*. That was a real fire in the castle. And there was nothing in the DNA of genetically altered clones to keep them from burning just like ordinary people.

What are we going to do . . . ?

Andy wasn't really asking her for an answer; he was just thinking out loud. But then Amy noticed something that gave her a response.

There's a paper stuck to the back of your shirt. She took it off and read it. *"You are in your element." Wait a minute— isn't that what the last message said too?*

Yeah. Your stupid friend must have stuck it on me

again. He snatched it out of her hands, crumpled it, and threw it into the fire.

Despite the immediate danger, she had to defend Chris. *Chris wouldn't play jokes at a time like this! That note must have meant something!*

Oh yeah? What did that note tell us that can get us out of this?

Amy had no answer. But she *did* catch a glimpse of something that looked clickable.

What's that thing by your foot?

Carefully, Andy crouched down. When a dancing flame threw light on the object, he was able to examine it. **It looks like a crank. There's some kind of faucet under it.**

A faucet could mean water. And water would douse the flames. *Can you turn it?*

With effort, Andy began to tug at the crank. It moved, but no water dripped out. Instead, what looked like a string emerged from the spout. Actually, it was a wire. It was stiff, and it extended straight out above the flames until they couldn't see it anymore.

I think we get to make a choice. He didn't sound thrilled about it.

What do you mean?

We can hang from the wire and try to get across hand over hand. Or we can try walking on it.

75

Neither option appealed to Amy. She did some rough estimating in her head. If they hung from the wire, the flames would be lapping at their feet. In Andy's case, since he was almost a foot taller than Amy, his feet would bear the full damage. On the other hand, walking a high wire had never been one of her great ambitions in life, and she'd certainly never trained for a circus profession. But their genetics did give them excellent balance.

I vote for walking.

Andy agreed. **All right. You go ahead of me. I can catch you if you start to fall.**

Great, Amy thought. Then we can both fall together. She conjured up a memory of the last circus she had been to and tried to capture the image of a tightrope walker. She copied the stance she saw in her mind— back straight, head up, arms extended to either side. Slowly, she lifted her right foot, pointed her toes, and stepped.

The wire accepted her weight. Though she certainly didn't feel secure, she had no choice but to put pressure on that foot so she could lift the left one and move it in front of the right one. Now she had both feet on the wire. Holding her breath, she concentrated on balance and tried to block out the fire below.

It's no different from Rollerblading or ice-skating,

she told herself. And you're good at both of those. There's no reason why you can't make it to the end of this wire. She didn't want to think about what might be waiting for her there. The wire had to lead somewhere. Hadn't Chris told her there were no dead ends? There was always a way. And even if this so-called virtual reality had turned into *real* reality, surely all the rules of Darklands wouldn't have changed.

She was aware of Andy as he stepped onto the wire. He was being careful, but the wire wobbled a bit. Amy waved her arms and stayed on the wire. Inch by inch, refusing to look down or even think about what was below her, she moved along. She could feel Andy keeping pace behind her.

The heat from the fire was making her sweat. A drop of perspiration ran off her forehead and down her nose. It sat at the tip, and she didn't dare shake her head or rub it off. The sensation became almost unbearable, worse than the heat or the fear. It was like needing to pee when you were sitting on a bus and wondering if you could make it to the next stop. There was no way you could make yourself stop thinking about it.

But somehow, you made it to that next stop and the closest rest room, and what a relief it was. That was what it would be like for her here. She had to think about the relief she'd feel when she was safely beyond the fire and able to wipe the drop of sweat from her nose.

She wanted to ask Andy how he was doing, but she was afraid that speaking might throw off her balance. As long as she could feel him stepping behind her, she had to figure he was fine. And now . . . was it wishful thinking, or did the flames seem to be dying down a bit? It didn't seem quite as hot, and although she could still hear the crackling, the flames weren't coming up high enough for her to feel them. Was there an end in sight?

Yes. She could see it. It looked like solid ground too. That could be an illusion, she supposed. After all, a game like this was all about illusions. For all she knew, she was an illusion too. Right now, as she considered the possible plateau that seemed to be real, she might actually be safe in Chris's bedroom, playing the game. But she had to believe in something, so she chose to believe that safety lay just ahead. It gave her a focus.

Andy needed to know what was happening.

She spoke carefully, so as not to cause any vibrations. *Hang in there. Just a few more steps.*

But no sooner had the words left her lips than an ominous sound began. The whistle of an Intruder.

Andy heard it too. *It's behind me.*

Close?

No. But getting closer.

Amy didn't dare turn to look, and she knew Andy wouldn't either. Such a movement would surely upset their balance. All they could do was pick up the pace and hope to meet the Intruder on solid ground, where they could possibly do battle. Or run.

The whistle got louder, but the ground was getting closer. Mentally, Amy chanted, You can do it, you can do it, you can do it, at a rhythm that kept her pace steady. Her heart kept the rhythm too, beating faster and faster—sometimes so loudly it almost drowned out the sound of the approaching Intruder, but not quite. She was too aware. She half imagined she could already feel the chill.

But then she felt something else—solid ground. Yes, it was definitely real, solid ground, and she allowed herself the tiniest instant of relief. Then she whirled around to see how close Andy was behind her. He was close—but so was the Intruder. He practically loomed over Andy.

Amy thrust out her arm toward him. He extended his own arm, but the movement threw off his balance, and he swayed precariously. Risking her own safety, Amy leaned forward, grabbed his hand with both of her own, and pulled him forward. Then he too was on solid ground—but the Intruder was making its way there as well.

Moving quickly, Amy took the knife from her pocket, knelt down, and pressed it against the wire. The wire resisted, but she gritted her teeth and pressed harder, sawing back and forth. The Intruder was close, too close, and now she really could feel the chill. She didn't know if it was fear or determination that kept her hacking away at the wire—a combination of the two, probably. Whatever it was, it worked. The knife cut through the wire. She let the end drop and held her breath as she watched to see the effect on the Intruder.

There was a hollow, unearthly scream as the creature fell into the flames. For a moment, it occurred to Amy that earlier, the Intruder had seemed to float above the ground. So why had he fallen when the wire he rested on had been cut? That was what she didn't like about computer games—things weren't logical.

They looked down at the flames. There was no sign of the Intruder, but that didn't give them room to relax. There would always be another one.

Holding hands, they moved through the darkness, smoke and rubble all that remained of the castle. Andy was the first to see something interesting. "There, on the floor. It's a design."

It looked like an ancient mosaic of some sort, embedded in the castle floor. Amy knelt down to get a closer look.

It's a circle with a plus sign inside. Is that a symbol?

It looks like a witchcraft thing. A circle divided into four parts.

Amy remembered a movie she'd seen about four teenage witches. They had a ritual in which each girl represented a direction. *Could it mean north, south, east, west?*

Maybe. Or it could be seasons. Summer, fall, winter, spring. It could be anything that comes in fours.

Gingerly, Amy touched each quadrant to see if any was clickable. Nothing happened. Then it has to be a clue, she thought.

It's telling us something.

I don't hear anything.

Ha ha, very funny. Get serious, Andy. Don't you want to get to level three?

I don't care about the next level. I just want to get out of here.

Like I don't? You're *the one who said we had to hide from the organization, remember? You're the one who said we were in danger.*

Yeah, well, I didn't know this stupid game would be even more dangerous. I didn't know your friend Chris was out to get us!

Just shut up about Chris, okay? Look for some way to get out of this castle.

How about a door?

Amy wished she could kick the sarcasm out of him. But there *was* a door. Two doors, in fact.

Which one?

Andy moved to one door and opened it to reveal a road made of yellow bricks. He went to the opposite side of the room and opened the other door to find a dirt path.

This one.

Why?

Because the other one is paved. It looks too easy. It's a setup.

How do you know? I like the yellow brick road. It reminds me of The Wizard of Oz.

No, this is the way we're going. Come on.

You're not in charge here!

Are you?

We should be making decisions together.

Amy, I don't feel like hanging around here to discuss this. I'm taking the dirt path.

Well, I'm taking the yellow brick road.

Do what you want. Say hi to the Tin Man for me.

Amy turned away from him and started for the door. Surely, Andy wouldn't let her walk out there alone. At the last minute, he'd come running after her.

But he didn't. She couldn't believe it. He was deserting her. Furious, she turned around and saw that he'd already stepped out onto the path. That was when she saw something else. Something stuck to the back of his pants.

Andy, wait!

At least he had the decency to stop. She went over and took the paper off his backside. *"You are in your element,"* she read out loud.

Not that *again.*

But suddenly it made sense. *Andy, that's it!*

What?

The elements! There are four of them, right? Earth, air, fire, and water. We conquered water by going under the moat. We just escaped fire. We've got earth and air left.

Andy looked down. **That's earth. At least, that's what it's supposed to be. So I'm right. This is the way to go.**

Amy had to agree, but she couldn't resist pointing out one thing. I'm *the one who figured out* why.

n**9**ne

The dirt path twisted and turned, but it didn't present any major challenge right away. There was nothing much to look at—just dirt, with the occasional artistically placed rock. The weather wasn't remarkable, neither hot nor cold. Amy and Andy walked along in silence. They weren't arguing, but echoes of their earlier disagreements hung in the air. They were still side by side, but they had stopped holding hands a while back.

Every now and then, Amy sneaked a peek at him. Funny, how little she really knew about Andy. They'd never really talked much about their pasts, their families, their feelings about being who they were. She'd always felt they didn't need to talk about these things—that they were soul mates who just understood each other automatically. But now she wondered. Would real soul mates bicker and argue and get on each other's nerves like this?

Was Andy having these thoughts too? She had to know.

Andy, how do you feel about me?

There was no response. He didn't even look at her. Then she realized she hadn't even heard her own voice.

Andy? Andy, do you hear me?

No, he wasn't just ignoring her. He couldn't hear her, because her voice made no sound. It dawned on her that she hadn't heard anything for a while. None of the usual sound effects were audible. On an impulse, Amy bent down, picked up a stone, and threw it toward a large rock. She could see the stone hit the rock, but it didn't make any noise.

Andy noticed. He looked at her, opened his mouth, and moved his lips. But no words came out. She could see from his expression that he was just as puzzled as she was.

She read his lips as he asked, **What's going on?**

Considering the situation, she came up with a possible explanation.

Someone's clicked on Mute. They cut off the program's sound.

Andy looked at her as if she was talking absolute nonsense. Annoyed, she asked, *You got a better idea?*

He continued to stare. That was when she realized he couldn't read lips. Why had she assumed he could? Just because *she* could? They didn't have ESP; they weren't psychic twins; they weren't *exactly* alike. What were they to each other, anyway?

With her finger, she wrote the word *mute* in the dirt. When he still looked confused, she wrote *program*. Then he nodded in comprehension. Making a shrugging motion, he seemed to be saying there was nothing they could do about it. She nodded in agreement, and they stopped trying to communicate.

Maybe it was just as well that the program had been muted. Amy didn't really want to talk about their relationship, and now she had an excuse to be silent.

She looked ahead. All she saw was the long, winding road. There were no buildings, no mountains, nothing that looked like something to be conquered. Maybe they'd made the wrong decision. Maybe she hadn't been right about the elements being the key. Maybe they were destined to wander silently down a road in a computer program forever and ever.

Suddenly, she was more frightened than she'd been since the beginning of their adventure. She could feel tears spring into her eyes, and she blinked furiously, trying to make them go away. She didn't want Andy to see how truly scared she was. Then she turned to him, because she *wanted* him to see the tears. She wanted him to comfort her.

But he didn't even notice. He was staring straight ahead. She supposed she could touch his arm to get his attention. But what if he just stared at her coldly anyway? She shivered. She imagined she could already feel the chill from his eyes.

No, not from his eyes. As the chill gripped her all over, she realized in horror what she was really feeling. She was being attacked by an Intruder.

There had been no warning this time, no whistling sound—but of course, there couldn't be, since the program had been muted. She caught only a glimpse of the horrible creature, because now she was frozen all over.

She couldn't even move her lips. *Andy, help me!* But the scream was only in her head. Andy kept on walking. He had no idea what had happened to her.

Horrified, she watched as he continued down the dirt path. How could he not know that she wasn't by his side any longer? Was she that unimportant to him?

She was so cold, so cold. Frozen all the way through—she was an ice stone, unable to call out or signal. She didn't even think she was breathing. But she must have been, because her heartbeat quickened when she saw Andy stop in his tracks. He turned.

Now he was running back to her. But what could he do for her? How could she be melted? There was no fire, no sign of anything that could provide warmth. Except his arms. He wrapped them around her frozen body and pulled her to the ground. And they lay there, their bodies pressed so tightly together that she thought she could feel his heart through the ice that encased her body.

Amy began to melt. She even began to feel the heat of Andy's skin. And there was absolutely nothing sexy about it. She loved him. She knew he loved her, but it wasn't romantic love. It was like having a brother and being a sister. And despite the fact that she was still very, very cold, she was warm all over, knowing she'd finally figured out who they were to each other. Everything made sense—the connection they felt, the ideas they shared, even the way they'd been sniping at each other. Like brother and sister.

How do you feel?

Cold. Hey, I heard you!

I guess someone put the sound back on. Can you walk?

I think so.

Andy helped her up. She was stiff, but she could put one foot in front of the other.

One thing I don't understand. Chris told me if the Intruder obliterated you, then the game had to start over. How come we're still alive and still in the same place?

Because we don't belong here. We're human. Humans aren't supposed to be inside computer programs. The rules don't apply to us.

Some of the rules apply. Like, we still have to click on things to make them happen.

I know that. I'm just saying that it's different for us, for real people, than it is for the characters in these games. Some rules apply and some rules don't.

But which ones?

If I knew that, we'd be out of here already!

There was no way she could miss the irritability in his voice, but this time it didn't bother her at all. Now that she could think of him as family, it was all right for him to snap at her. They were in this together.

They continued to walk, and still, Amy couldn't see anything looming in the distance that could possibly become their earth-element problem. It wasn't long, however, before she realized why. The earth problem didn't lie ahead. It lay underneath.

The tremor was almost imperceptible at first, like a quiver, a little bump in the ground. Amy turned to Andy, and she could see in his face that he felt it too. The tremor grew in intensity, slowly but steadily, as if whoever was playing the game was increasing the power number on the Richter scale deliberately.

Earthquake.

Not very realistic.

She agreed. Both she and Andy were Californians. They knew what earthquakes were all about. This one was too even, too smooth, too . . .

Too dramatic. There was an enormous snapping sound. A smooth crack appeared in the ground between them. The earth began to separate.

Andy reached out to Amy as she tried to leap over the fissure. Their hands touched, but that didn't do either of them much good. They tumbled into the opening.

It was like falling in slow motion. It wasn't all that terrifying to Amy, because it felt more like she was floating downward with a parachute that would keep her from going too fast or from hitting the ground with a devastating thud. And they *did* land gently—in a pit full of snakes.

Amy knew there was no reason to be afraid. These weren't real snakes. But she'd never liked them, not even when they were behind glass at the zoo. She couldn't move; she felt almost as stiff as she had when she was covered with ice.

Once again, she had to count on Andy. He gripped her hand and pulled her along. He kicked snakes out of the way and stopped to dig in the dirt with his bare hands. At first he tried to carve a tunnel for them to move through, but the ground shifted, so he piled dirt to form hills for them to climb.

But it wasn't working. A snake raced past them, moving upward toward some surface they couldn't see.

We have to follow the snakes. They know the way out.

Andy burrowed into the dirt in the direction of the last snake. Amy tried to help. But every time she put her hands into the dirt, another snake appeared and she jumped back. She was so ashamed to be dependent on Andy to take charge. They were supposed to be perfect, she and Andy. She shouldn't be showing an illogical fear like this. There was a reason for these snakes to be here. They were guides. Only they moved so fast, she and Andy couldn't keep up with them.

Andy . . . what if we grabbed on to a snake and let it pull us out?

Okay. How about if I grab a snake and you grab me?

If they hadn't been practically buried underground, she would have hugged him. He saw her fear, understood it, and was helping her find a way around it. She would do the same for him. Maybe showing a weakness was a way of letting someone know how much he was trusted.

Andy grabbed the tail of the next snake, and Amy grabbed Andy's legs. They were pulled upward through a tunnel in the dirt and found themselves up on the ground. The snake had disappeared.

They were facing a building. A dozen doors led into it, and Amy knew the choice of doors had to be important.

Andy was staring up, even though there was nothing above him. *We must be in level four. The next challenge has to be air.*

I think we need to get into this building.

Why?

Because it's here. We have to pick a door to enter.

They all look alike.

There are numbers on them. That has to mean something. But the numbers didn't follow any consecutive order. They were all three digits—462, 893, 221 . . . there didn't seem to be any logic to the sequences. She and Andy stared at them, trying to come up with some sort of pattern, but nothing came to either of them.

Did we see any numbers earlier? I don't remember any.

Amy did. She reached into her pocket and pulled out

93

the coin she'd fished out of the fountain. *Seven forty-nine,* she said. *Is there a door with that number on it?*

There was, at the other end of the building. But they didn't have to walk to it. They were moved to the door by an unseen force.

What was that?

Someone clicked on us! Chris must be back in control. She reached for the door handle, but Andy grabbed her hand.

This could be a trick. He could be setting us up for something.

No way. Chris wouldn't do that. She shook her hand free and turned the handle.

The door opened. Total blackness. There was no way of knowing what lay over the threshold.

What's that?

Where?

But Andy wasn't looking inside the room. He was watching the sky. *That. Those birds.*

They're nothing, just background. Okay, should we go in together?

Andy wasn't listening. *Birds fly through the air.*

Yeah, that's brilliant, Andy. Come on, together or one at a time?

We're not going inside. We're going to grab on to a

bird. Like we did with the snake. We grabbed it, and it carried us through the earth. The birds will carry us through the air.

You can't access the birds, Andy. I tried when I was playing the game with Chris. Nothing happens when you click on them.

Nothing happened when you were with Chris. Big surprise. He probably did something so the birds wouldn't work.

Andy, stop it. Stop criticizing Chris.

I'm just saying you can't trust him.

How can you say that? You've never even met him!

I don't need to meet him. We can't trust anyone who isn't one of us.

That's crazy! Are you saying I can't have friends who aren't genetically altered clones?

You can have any friends you want, just don't trust them.

What about my mother? She isn't a genetically altered clone.

Remember, I couldn't trust my father.

Amy couldn't argue with him about that. How awful it must have been for him to discover that his father was aligned with the organization. But to not trust the people she cared about deeply . . . to not trust her mother, Tasha, Chris . . . even Eric, because in the long run, no matter how obnoxious he got or how mad he was at her, she knew he wouldn't betray her . . . it seemed awfully sad.

Are you going with me?

A bird was swooping down near them. Andy prepared to leap. He extended his hand for Amy to grab.

But Amy wouldn't put her hand in his. She knew that Chris had directed her to this door, and she was going in. Maybe once Andy realized he couldn't grab on to the bird, he'd come with her.

But Andy *did* get his hands on the bird. She watched in astonishment as he flew off with it. He was gone.

She turned back to the door and stepped into the darkness.

ten 10

A cool wind brushed against Amy's face. It was as if she was running into the wind, even though she wasn't making herself move. Then the wind went into reverse, and she had the sensation of being sucked into a vacuum cleaner. The wind was pulling her inside. She couldn't see, she couldn't hear, and she had no idea where she was going. But it seemed right. She knew she was leaving Darklands, and she felt no fear.

Still, when the darkness opened into light, she was startled to find herself on the floor in Eric's bedroom.

Eric gaped at her. Clearly, he was just as surprised as she was.

"What are *you* doing here?" he asked.

"That's what I'd like to know," she said, getting up and dusting off her jeans. There was nothing to dust off, but she could still feel the dirt she'd crawled through. "How did you get me out of there?"

"Out of where?"

"Darklands, dummy!"

His mouth dropped open. "You were inside the game?"

She nodded. "So was Andy. That's where he went to hide. Chris helped me get inside the game, and I ran into Andy there." As she spoke, she realized how insane she sounded. She was talking like she'd just run into Andy at a shopping mall or movie. "Anyway, that's where I've been all this time. Inside Darklands."

"What do you mean, 'all this time'? You left here only an hour ago."

She was amazed. True, she'd had no sense of time in Darklands. She realized now she hadn't experienced hunger or thirst or the desire to sleep. But it was incredible to think about all that had happened within the short time frame of one hour.

She went over to Eric's desk and examined his computer screen. It was blank. "Weren't you playing?"

"I tried to," he said, sounding annoyed. "But I couldn't click on anything, and the image kept changing. Little

98

sound blips were driving me crazy. I had to click on mute."

Amy glared at him. "So that was you. An Intruder got me because I couldn't hear it."

"Sorry, but how was I supposed to know it was you? All I saw was a semicolon. Or sometimes a period and a comma."

Amy wondered which one had been her. It was very strange to think she'd been reduced to a punctuation mark.

"The marks were running all over the screen," Eric continued. "You ever spill anything on a keyboard?"

"No," Amy said. "I'm not a slob. I know better than to eat or drink while I'm working on a PC."

Eric ignored the implied insult. "It completely messes up the keyboard. Like, one letter or number or symbol will keep repeating itself across the screen, and you can't stop it."

"Were you drinking something?"

"Just some orange juice." He sounded defensive. "It wasn't like a soda or anything with bubbles."

"I don't think the health value of the drink has anything to do with the kind of damage it can do to a computer," Amy pointed out. "It was your stupid orange juice that put me and Andy in so much danger!"

"I didn't spill it! At least, I don't think I did. Anyway,

I tried to get rid of the marks but the delete key wouldn't work. Once that semicolon appeared, nothing worked."

"Thank goodness for that," Amy remarked. She couldn't imagine what would have happened if Eric had deleted the semicolon Amy/Andy.

"So I figured the CD was damaged," Eric said.

"Let me look at it."

Eric obliged. He pressed a button on the side of the computer, and the CD drive opened. Amy went to take it out of the slot.

"Hey, hold it by the edges," Eric ordered her. "Don't smudge it."

"I know how to hold a CD," Amy informed him. Gingerly, she removed the disc and examined it. "I don't see any scratches or smudges."

"You can't always see a scratch," Eric pointed out.

Amy rolled her eyes. Had Eric forgotten what kind of extraordinary vision she had? "*I* can. I don't think there's anything wrong with this disc. Not on the outside, at least. Can you get back into the game?"

Eric took the disc from her with his free hand and inserted it. Amy watched impatiently while he fumbled with keys. She wanted to whip the keyboard out of his hands and do it herself.

Anxiety was creeping up on her. If Eric hadn't been

playing Darklands and putting them in those situations, who had been? And where was Andy now?

"Hurry up," she urged him.

"I'm moving as fast as I can," he told her. "It's not easy with one hand, you know."

"Just click on that arrow," Amy said, and before Eric could stop her, she snatched the mouse and clicked on it herself.

Eric groaned. "Oh, great, Amy. Now we have to sit through the entire introduction. I could have skipped over it, but now it's too late."

"Sorry," Amy said sheepishly.

"Just because I'm not a genetically altered clone doesn't mean I'm an idiot," he added.

"I never said you were an idiot," Amy objected.

"Sure you did. Not with words, maybe. But I could tell. I knew you'd always be superior to me, in every way, and it was hard enough to live with that. But for an ordinary human being . . . I'm not so pathetic."

For a moment, Amy forgot about Darklands and Andy and everything that had happened in the past hour. "Oh, no, Eric! You're not pathetic, not at all. Did I really make you feel that way?"

"Sometimes," he admitted.

Shame swept over her. She didn't even try to defend herself because she knew what he said was true.

It couldn't have been easy for him, having a girlfriend like her.

She glanced at the screen. The introduction was still under way—swirls of colors, eerie music, lots of names. She turned back to Eric.

"I'm sorry," she said.

He thought she was talking about her computer snafu. "It's okay. The game will start in about a minute."

"No, I mean, about us, about the way I made you feel."

He shrugged. "Yeah, okay. Whatever."

Amy wasn't finished. "I was being very dense. And dumb. I'll admit it. But you haven't been so nice to me lately. Ever since you started high school, you've been acting like you're too good for me now."

"Hey, that's completely different," Eric pointed out.

"How so?"

He grinned. "Because I'm naturally dense. And dumber than you. So I have an excuse."

She grabbed a pillow off his bed and threw it at him. He was about to return the gesture when he noticed the computer screen had changed. "It's starting."

They both studied the screen. It displayed a beach scene—sand, the ocean, foam on the crests of the waves.

"I didn't see this when I was in Darklands," Amy said.

"That's level one. You probably went in at level two. That's where Chris was."

"So what's the element here?"

"It's water. You get two chances to conquer that, here and in the moat."

It was then that Amy noticed something odd about the scene compared to the other Darklands images. There were no sound effects. She should have been able to hear the crashing of the waves.

"Is it on mute?"

Eric checked the panel at the lower right-hand corner. "No."

"Why aren't the waves moving?"

"That's what I've been trying to tell you. Something's wrong with the game."

"I didn't see anything wrong with the disc," Amy recalled. "Is it possible that you contracted a computer virus?"

"It's possible," Eric acknowledged. "Maybe Andy infected it when he went into the game."

"Or you caught it online," Amy said. "Were you surfing the Net today?"

"No, and I haven't sent any e-mails, either."

Amy snapped her fingers. "Instant messages."

Eric nodded. "Yeah, that's right. I was instant messaging Chris this morning, about setting up the network. If Chris had a virus, I could have caught it from him." He frowned. "I'm wondering . . ."

"What?"

"If maybe your hoodlum friend didn't give it to me on purpose."

Amy clutched her head. "Will you cut it out? He's not a hoodlum!"

"Then why didn't he zap the Intruders? Why did you and Andy get into so much trouble?"

She defended Chris. "If he's got the virus too, he wasn't able to play the game any more than you were."

"Amy . . ." Eric looked at her intently. "I'm not just knocking your guy. This game can't do anything by itself. If no one operates it, nothing happens. Someone was playing this game. And it wasn't me."

"Millions of people play Darklands," Amy reminded him.

"But they didn't have you and Andy on their discs," he argued. "You don't play this game online. You're not connected with other people while you're playing . . . unless . . ."

"Unless what?"

"Unless you're in a network with someone. Then you can share everything on your disc."

Amy went white. She reached for Eric's phone and dialed.

"Are you calling Chris?"

She nodded. Then she hung up. "It's busy."

"Maybe he's online," Eric said.

"Let's go," she said.

She could have run to Chris's house much faster on her own. But she knew that this wasn't a good time to demonstrate her superior running skills in front of Eric. Besides, she pondered things especially well when she walked, and she had a lot to ponder.

There had to be an explanation for this, a reasonable explanation. Too bad she couldn't come up with one. All she could hear was Andy's voice accusing Chris of being in league with the organization, telling Amy she couldn't trust anyone normal.

Andy's wrong, she told herself. He was wrong about not trusting people. He was wrong when he said people like us couldn't have ordinary friends. He was wrong about lots of things.

He was wrong about Chris too; he had to be. But the tiniest shadow of doubt was creeping through her mind now.

At the Martin house, Eric said, "Amy, let me handle this."

"Why?"

"Because I'm more objective. You're too involved with this guy. I'll be better equipped to know if he's telling the truth."

"Okay," Amy said reluctantly.

"Stay out of sight," Eric told her.

She didn't much like taking orders from him. But maybe it would be good to let Eric take charge once in a while. She went to the tree on the side of the house and hid behind the huge trunk. She could hear and see, but she was hidden from view to whoever opened the door.

Eric rang the doorbell, and Mrs. Martin opened it almost immediately. She didn't wear the welcoming smile Amy was used to seeing on her face.

"Who are you?" Mrs. Martin asked sharply.

"Eric Morgan. I'm a friend of Chris's. Is he home?"

"No. He's not here."

"Do you know what time he'll be back?" Eric asked politely.

"No . . . ," the woman sighed. "I don't know if he'll ever be back."

"What do you mean?" Eric asked.

"Chris has run away from home! His clothes are gone! Do you know his friend Amy Candler? I haven't been able to reach her. She might know where Chris went."

"Um, I don't know where Amy is," Eric said. "Or Chris."

Mrs. Martin was clearly upset. "I don't understand this! The social service people warned me he might do something like this. They said he wasn't used to the stability of family life and a home. But I thought things were going so well!" She was talking more to herself than to Eric, and Eric just nodded politely.

"Are you sure he ran away?" he asked her. "Is it possible that someone could have abducted him?"

"I don't see how, or why," Mrs. Martin replied. "And I don't think kidnappers normally let the victim pack their favorite things and take a backpack. His pack is gone, and his favorite sneakers, and his leather jacket, and—"

Eric interrupted. "His laptop? Did he take his computer with him?"

As she watched from her position behind the tree, Amy saw Mrs. Martin nod, and she could feel her own heart breaking.

eleven

"Where do you think he could have gone?" Eric asked Amy as they walked home.

"Not a clue," she said. "Before he came to live with the Martins, Chris stayed in homeless shelters."

"Where does he hang out?"

"I don't know," she said honestly. "He doesn't have any good friends. Besides me." And now he doesn't even have me, she added silently, in an effort to harden her heart.

Eric was grim. "Wherever he is, he's got his laptop. Which means he could still be playing Darklands."

"And Andy's still inside," Amy said. She shuddered. "I

can't imagine what Chris might be doing to him." Her voice broke.

Eric studied her thoughtfully. "You really like Andy, don't you?" His voice was wistful. "I could tell, the first time you met him, back at Wilderness Adventure. You care about him a lot."

"Of course I do," Amy said. "Just like I care about all my friends. Like I care about you, and . . . well, like I *used* to care about Chris. Just because I like a guy and care about him and want to save his life doesn't mean I'm madly in love with him, you know."

"Really?"

She groaned. "Eric, we've got more important things to worry about than my love life." She could have been addressing herself with those words. She had to stop thinking about Chris and his betrayal and concentrate on getting Andy out of Darklands.

"Let's get your disc and put it in my computer," she said.

"But if the disc's infected, it won't work there either," Eric pointed out.

"But if the problem's in your hard drive, it might," she argued.

They went back to Eric's and got the disc. At Amy's, Monica and Sunshine were at the dinner table, working on the embroidery. Monica waved cheerfully.

"Hi! What have you been up to this morning?"

If she hadn't been so worried about Andy, Amy would have laughed. "Nothing much," she said.

Sunshine looked at her. "Have you taken any journeys?"

Amy blinked. Then she stared hard at the strange girl. "What do you mean?"

"Every day, one should take a journey," Sunshine said solemnly. "A voyage of self-discovery. A spiritual journey, to some remote point in your inner self, a journey of discovery, of—"

"No thanks," Amy interrupted. "I've had all the adventures I want today. C'mon, Eric." They went upstairs to her bedroom.

"What a weirdo," Eric commented.

"No kidding. I can't believe I thought she might be an organization spy." She turned on her PC and hit the button to open the CD-ROM player. Eric positioned the disc, and Amy let him take charge. This time, she let him override the introduction so they could get straight to the opening scene of the game.

It was the beach again, level one. But this time, the waves were in motion, with full sound effects. Watching over Eric's shoulder, Amy scanned the scene for signs of a semicolon or a period or a comma. "I don't see Andy," she said.

"He's not going to be there," Eric said. "Where was he when you left?"

"We had just come out of the snake pit. He grabbed on to a bird and flew off. Chris told me you couldn't access birds."

"Not till level three," Eric informed her.

She supposed she had to be fair and believe that Chris hadn't known this, since he'd been stuck in level two. On the other hand, maybe he had known and had just told her that to make sure she and Andy would separate.

Eric was using the mouse to push the cursor around the screen. He frowned. "It's not responding. We're not going to be able to move."

"I don't understand."

"It's the disc. He's put some kind of bug in the program."

"Wait," Amy said. "What's happening now?"

They were no longer on the beach. Images flashed across the screen—the garden, the fountain, the moat, the castle. But Eric's good hand wasn't even on the mouse.

Now the image was unfamiliar—a spaceship on a landing pad. At the base of the ship, sparks were flying; the rocket appeared ready for liftoff. Then a bird appeared, flying toward the spaceship. Amy focused on it.

"Can you see anything?" Eric asked her.

"There's a dark speck on the bird. It might be a period." Which would mean it was Andy. On the other hand, she couldn't remember the last time she'd cleaned the screen. She rubbed the spot with her finger. Nothing came off.

"Try clicking on the bird," Amy suggested.

"It won't do any good," Eric said. He tried anyway, but he was right. "See? We can watch and see what happens, but we can't do anything."

A window in the spaceship opened, and the bird flew in. A second later, it flew out, but this time, Amy couldn't see any spot on it. "Andy's in the spaceship," she said.

"Yeah, that's what I think too." Eric sounded worried. "Look, the sparks aren't flying. Everything's stopped."

"What does that mean?"

"I never got to this level," Eric admitted. "But I'll bet you have to take specific actions to make the rocket blast off. You probably have to go inside and play with the dials. There might even be codes. This is how people get trapped in a level. They haven't picked up the right information to make something happen."

"You think Chris got stuck here?"

Eric nodded. "The game gets harder and harder. I know a guy who's spent a year working through these levels, and he hasn't finished yet."

Amy gazed at the screen in dismay and thought of Andy, stuck in that spaceship for a year. Maybe forever.

"And if Chris is a really rotten guy, it could get worse for Andy," Eric said. "He could take him out of the spaceship and make stuff happen to him."

"What kind of stuff?" Amy asked anxiously.

"You don't want to know."

Now she was feeling really sick. "Eric, we have to find Chris. We have to take control of this game and get Andy out."

Eric agreed. "But how are we going to find Chris? He could be anywhere. We could call the police, but what are we going to tell them? This guy has a friend of ours locked up in a computer game? I don't think they're going to buy that."

Amy was thinking. "Something just occurred to me. Your computer isn't the only one in your house, right?"

"My parents have one, and Tasha has her own."

"Are they connected?"

"We have a family network thing," Eric said. "Mainly for a calendar. So people can enter appointments and plans, stuff like that, so everyone knows where everyone else is."

"That's what I thought," Amy said. "Lots of families have home networks like that. Maybe the Martins do too. And if they do, maybe we can use one of their other computers to stop Chris and get Andy out."

Eric looked doubtful. "I don't know if it works like that."

"It's worth a try," Amy pleaded. "Think about it, Eric. Would you want to be stuck in a computer game for a year? Even if it was Darklands?"

Eric considered this. "Not with that hoodlum telling me what to do. Come on, let's go back to the Martins'."

twelve
12

"Try again," Amy said.

Eric pressed the buzzer. Then he knocked, hard and loud. But no one came to the Martins' door.

"That's odd," Amy said. "Their car is here. If they were out looking for Chris, they'd have taken the car."

"They could have gone for a walk," Eric said.

"Eric, this is Los Angeles. Nobody walks here. And if they're not out looking for Chris in a car, they would be sitting by the phone, hoping he'd call."

"Maybe they have a cell phone," Eric suggested.

Amy rolled her eyes. She wasn't in the mood for

logic. "Maybe they're just not answering the door. Maybe they're depressed about Chris."

Eric looked skeptical. Amy put her hand on the doorknob and gave it a twist. "It's locked."

"Of course it's locked," Eric said.

Amy studied the door. "I wonder if I could force the lock."

"Amy, are you crazy? You can't break into people's houses!"

Amy turned to him. "Eric, I can't leave Andy in that game! I don't know why Chris has trapped him in there or what he's going to do to him. We have to get him out! And I don't care if I have to break a law to do it!" She started walking around the house. "Maybe there's a window open."

Eric followed her. He even went around to check if the back door was locked. It was, and so were the windows on the first floor of the house. Amy gazed up toward the second floor.

She caught her breath. "Eric, do you see that?"

"What?"

"The window in the middle, behind the leaves of the tree. That's Chris's room. I see a shadow behind the curtain."

Eric squinted. "Are you sure? I don't see anything."

Amy wasn't sure—but she wasn't about to leave any stone unturned. She leaped up and grabbed the closest branch of the tree. She scrambled up till she was level with the window. Now she was sure. There was definitely someone in the room.

She hesitated. It had to be one of the Martins. What was she going to do? She wasn't even sure she could make it to the window. No ordinary person could jump that far.

Of course, she could jump farther than normal people, but there would be no buildup to her leap. She could end up crashing to the ground.

And if she even made it to the window, then what would she do? Rap on the glass and demand to be given access to a computer? Was she really going to intrude on their grief like this? She wished she could think of another way.

Then the curtain fluttered. A hand appeared, and then a face. Amy was in shock.

Chris looked just as stunned. He jerked the window open. "What are you doing?" he asked nervously. "Get out of here!"

"No way, Jose," she replied. The sight of Chris gave her the emotional momentum she needed. She leaped, and just barely managed to get her fingertips on the upper edge of the window. Then she kicked her legs out and knocked Chris down to the floor as she swung herself into his bedroom. While he was still on the floor, Amy leaped onto him and pinned his arms down.

"Where's Andy? What have you done with him?"

"Are you nuts?" he yelled. "Hey, you're hurting me!"

"Tell me where Andy is!" she shrieked.

"Shut up, they'll hear you!" he cried out. He strained to break free from her grip, but he was no match for her. "It wasn't me!"

Furious, she dragged him upright, pushed him face-down down on his bed, and pulled his arms tightly behind his back. He let out a howl of pain.

"Tell me where Andy is or I'll break your arm!" she demanded.

"I think you already did," he moaned.

She realized she would have to tie him up so her hands would be free to work on his computer. Wildly, she looked around for something to use as a rope. That was when she realized the computer wasn't on his desk.

"Where's the computer?"

His face was now pressed so hard into the mattress that his reply was muffled, but she caught the word *downstairs*. Pushing him aside, she ran to his closed door and turned the knob. Nothing happened. The door had been locked.

Now on the floor, Chris gasped, "They took the computer and locked me in!"

"Who did? The organization?"

"My foster parents!" he moaned.

"What?"

"The Martins! They're the bad guys! They're playing Darklands on the dining room table!"

As if in confirmation, a voice called out from below, "Shut up! Stop yelling or we'll put *you* in this game too!" It was the voice of Mrs. Martin.

Amy gathered her strength and kicked the door. With a loud crack, it broke open, and she ran out, flying down the stairs. She knew the Martins had heard the commotion and she was prepared to take them both on. What she wasn't prepared for was the sight of Mr. Martin in the archway leading to the dining room. He was beaming at her.

"She's here!" he yelled over his shoulder. "It's okay, you can let the spaceship explode!"

The Darklands sound effects were on, loud and clear. From the bottom of the stairs, Amy could hear the explosion.

thirteen 13

Amy pushed Mr. Martin aside, sending him crashing against the wall, and rushed to the computer. Mrs. Martin jumped up and stepped back. Amy got a clear view of the screen.

The visual effects of Darklands were as good as the sound effects. On screen, the shattered pieces of the rocket were like fireworks, colorful shards shooting out all over the screen. Amy froze. Some of those pieces had to be Andy.

She knew how vulnerable she must be right that moment. Grief overwhelmed her. The Martins could easily have subdued her.

But they didn't even try. Mrs. Martin actually looked happy to see her. Mr. Martin didn't even mind having been thrown against the wall. Rubbing a spot on his head, he approached Amy with a big smile.

"You're all right! Thank goodness!"

"We thought you might be in that spaceship," Mrs. Martin explained. "I was doing everything I could to keep it from taking off. We knew it would explode, and we couldn't figure out how to get you out."

In utter disbelief and confusion, Amy stared at them. "But someone *was* in that spaceship! Andy!"

Mrs. Martin brushed that aside. "He's not our responsibility. *You're* the one we care about." From the expression on her face, Amy got the feeling she was supposed to be pleased and flattered to hear this. She was too stunned to feel anything.

"What's going on here!" she shrieked.

"Now, now, dear, there's no need to scream," Mrs. Martin said reprovingly. "We're not going to hurt you. We're here to take care of you."

"Who are you?" Amy demanded. "Where do you come from? The organization?"

Mr. Martin nodded. "We were assigned to watch you, to make sure you didn't suffer any side effects from the implant."

"The implant," Amy repeated. "So there *is* a chip in my head."

"*Was*," Mrs. Martin corrected her. "When you put yourself into that silly game, it was disabled. We've been going crazy trying to keep an eye on you! Mr. Martin and I are from an older generation, you know. We're not as adept at these things as you young people are."

Amy's head was spinning, rendering her momentarily speechless. A sound behind her made her turn. Chris was approaching, looking just as stunned as she was as he cradled the arm she'd twisted.

Mr. Martin glanced at him without much interest. "This is why we took Chris on as a foster child," he explained. "So we'd have an excuse to be close to you."

Amy was still looking at Chris. "So—so you didn't know about this."

He shook his head. "I guess I should have been suspicious. Why would anyone want a homeless teenage hoodlum living in their house?" He winced. Amy wasn't sure if that came from the emotional pain of learning he wasn't wanted or the physical pain of his arm.

The sound of shattering glass made everyone jump. Less than a second later, Eric bounded into the room. He stopped and stared at them all.

"Who are *you*?" Mr. Martin demanded.

"Eric. Eric Morgan." He was rubbing his fist against his chest. "Man, that double-glazing isn't easy to break with one arm. What's going on here?"

Amy spoke flatly. "They're from the organization. Not Chris," she added hastily as Eric made a threatening move in his direction. "Just *them*. They were supposed to be watching me."

"For your own safety and protection," Mrs. Martin said.

Amy had a hard time getting the next words out. "But not for Andy's safety and protection."

"He wasn't our responsibility," Mrs. Martin repeated. "Each clone has his or her own watcher. It's not our fault that Andy's watcher didn't keep him safe."

"You didn't even try to get him out of the spaceship," Amy murmured. "You let it explode while he was inside."

"You could have killed him!" Eric exclaimed.

"They did kill him, Eric!" Amy wailed. "There was no way he could have survived that explosion!"

"What are you talking about?" Eric said. "He's right there!"

A figure emerged from under the dining room table. Andy was shaken and confused—but alive. Amy rushed to his side. "Andy! Are you okay?"

"Yeah, I think so. Wow, it was a lot harder getting out

of that game than it was getting in. I was concentrating like crazy, and nothing happened. Then—boom! I was here."

"Boom," Amy repeated. "That's a good way to describe it." Overcome with relief and joy, she felt like laughing. They were all here, all her boys—Eric, Andy, and Chris. They were all alive, and they were all the good guys she'd wanted to believe they were. She wished she could stretch out her arms and hug them all simultaneously.

But there were still the Martins to contend with. Neither of them seemed particularly concerned about the situation. Amy found that extremely annoying. She advanced toward them. "As for you two . . . ," she began in her most threatening voice.

"Now, now, dear," Mrs. Martin said. "Don't be upset. The organization only wants the best for you."

"I'm sure they only want the best for Andy, too," Amy replied.

"True," Mr. Martin acknowledged. "I'm sure they'd like to keep all their Crescent clones safe and sound. Unfortunately, Andy's watchers were a little lax. They're lucky he survived. Otherwise, they would be in serious trouble with the organization."

Mrs. Martin turned to him. "As it is, I'm sure they'll be severely reprimanded."

"And what about you two?" Amy demanded. "You think the organization is going to be happy with *you*?"

"You're alive and well," Mr. Martin pointed out.

"Yeah, but that has nothing to do with you! You weren't able to stop me from getting into that game. And you were willing to let Andy be destroyed. Maybe he wasn't your responsibility, but you didn't even try to save him. You think the organization is going to appreciate that?"

Mrs. Martin spoke to Mr. Martin. "She has a point. I think we should contact them for directions."

At least now they were looking a little unnerved. Amy wished she could leave them with more than that—like maybe a dozen broken bones and a concussion. But she just wanted to get out of there.

The three boys followed her toward the door. Mr. Martin hurried after them. "No, you need to stay here, Amy! You boys can leave, but we need to talk to Amy." He put a restraining hand on her arm. "We want to take care of you! You have to stay!"

Now Amy had an excuse to hurt him. With one quick move, she twisted his arm and sent him to the floor, howling in pain.

"In your dreams," she said. "C'mon, guys. We're outta here."

f o u r t e e n
14

A my spoke into the phone. "Right. Two large pepper-oni, one medium everything, hold the anchovies, and a medium vegetarian." She gave her address, thanked the person on the other end, and hung up.

"Think that's enough?" Eric asked anxiously. "I'm really hungry."

"One of those pepperoni pizzas is reserved exclusively for you," Amy reassured him. "The vegetarian is for Sunshine and Monica, the everything is Andy's, and Chris and I will share the other pepperoni."

Andy opened the door. "How are you feeling, Chris?"

"Okay." Chris was pale, and with his arm in a cast and sling, he didn't look especially comfortable. But he didn't look too bad, either.

"Yo, bro," Eric greeted him, indicating their twin right arms. "How was the emergency room?"

"Not bad," Chris said. "They took me right away."

Amy looked at her watch. It had been a couple of hours since they'd left Chris's foster home. "Where have you been?"

"I stopped at the Martins'. They're gone."

Amy nodded. "I figured the organization wouldn't be too happy with them." She sighed. "I'm sure they'll come up with another watcher before long." She gazed out the window. "Maybe they already have. I keep seeing this man in a green car hanging around."

"Neighborhood Watch," Eric said.

"What?"

"It's this new community organization. People take turns watching for robbers and stuff." He joined Amy at the window. "That's Mr. Stuyvesant from a few blocks up. He's always volunteering to take shifts. Mom says it's because his wife drives him crazy when he wants to read in peace. Hey, here comes your baby-sitter and her wacko friend."

Amy made a face at him. "She's not a baby-sitter.

You know how my mother is. She doesn't like to leave me alone."

"That Monica is certainly doing a great job taking care of you," Chris said solemnly, and they all cracked up.

The oblivious Monica came in with Sunshine. "Ooh, a party!" she said happily when she saw the group.

"I've ordered pizzas," Amy told her. "Vegetarian for you, Sunshine."

"How did you know I was a vegetarian?" Sunshine asked in surprise.

"Just a guess."

Monica was looking at the twin injuries. "*Two* broken arms?"

"Yeah, it's a contagious condition," Eric joked.

Sunshine eyed them with concern. "You shouldn't be wearing casts. The arms need air, not plaster."

"Thanks for the advice," Chris said. "But I think I'll follow the doctor's instructions."

"Doctors don't know everything," Sunshine said. "Many illnesses can be cured through the sheer will of the patient. Personally, I believe that many illnesses today can be traced to computer use. Looking at those screens all day cannot be healthy."

Amy remembered something. "Sunshine, did you change the image on my screen saver?"

"Why yes, I did. I thought it would be better for you."

"And did you go through my drawers?"

"Oh no," Sunshine assured her. "Nothing like that. I just opened all the drawers and cabinets and closet doors in the house. You need to release angry spirits every once in a while. I always do that when I know I'll be spending time in a place. Did I neglect to close your drawers?"

Amy could feel her own angry spirit coming out. "You had no business poking around in my room, Sunshine!"

"You have to deal with hostility in your system, Amy. You need to meditate. I believe that meditation is the way to resolve all problems, mental and physical and—"

"Come on, Sunshine," Monica interrupted. "Let's meditate on our wall hanging. Then we can meditate over the pizzas." Obediently, Sunshine followed her into the dining room.

Eric laughed and turned to Chris. "You got that? All we have to do is meditate and we can cure ourselves. We could put the entire medical profession out of business."

"My will isn't all that strong," Chris said. "What about you, Amy? You never get sick, and if you get injured you heal fast. Does that have anything to do with your will?"

"I don't know," Amy admitted. "Andy, what do you think?"

"I'm not sure," Andy said. "There's a lot we don't know about ourselves." He sounded unusually pensive. "I thought we were just physically stronger and smarter than regular people. But that doesn't explain what happened today. Like, how *did* we get ourselves in and out of that game?"

"I don't know," Amy said again.

"Neither do I," Andy said, "but we *should* know. We need to take charge of our lives, Amy. You were just saying the organization would send another watcher. Well, I don't think we should sit around and wait for that to happen. We can't simply respond to what they do. We have to be proactive. We need to know what they're doing, why they put those chips in our head, what they're planning for us."

Eric looked confused. "But you already know that. They want to create a master race to take over the world, right?"

Andy nodded. "But why? And how? And who are they, anyway? I don't want to wait anymore. I want to confront them."

Amy looked at him. "How do you plan on doing that?"

"I'm going on a quest," Andy said. "A mission. Come with me, Amy. Let's go find them together. You and me. Now."

A silence fell over the room. Eric broke it. "You want Amy to leave home?"

Andy nodded. "We can take care of each other. Maybe we can contact other Amys and Andys. We could make a family."

"But I *have* a family," Amy said gently. "My mother."

"Jeez, she'd go nuts if you took off," Eric said.

Amy agreed. "I realize that your father turned out to be a bad guy, Andy. And I'm sorry. But I'm absolutely, positively sure that my mother is on my side. Nothing you could say would convince me she's not."

"But she can't save you," Andy protested. "She can't save the world! You and I, on the other hand, might be able to do that."

Amy was torn. "I know. And you want to do a good thing. But I can't go with you, Andy. I can't leave my mother."

Andy's face fell. But he nodded. "Yeah, I can understand that. If I had a decent mother or father, I'd probably feel the same way. I can go alone."

"Alone," Amy repeated. It was such a sad word. She couldn't bear the thought of her Andy wandering on his own. He could take care of himself, but what would he do for company?

Chris had been listening thoughtfully, and he spoke up. "Let me go with you."

Andy was surprised. "You?"

"*I* don't have a family. I'm on my own. And now I don't even have a place to live. Okay, I know I'm just an ordinary clone with no special powers, but I'm reasonably strong and smart for a normal person. I'd be better than no one."

"Are you serious?" Andy asked him.

"Absolutely."

"But we've just met. I don't even know you." Andy turned to Amy. "You know this guy. What do you think?"

Now Amy was even more torn. She hated the thought of Chris's leaving. She wouldn't be seeing him at school, they wouldn't be hanging out, she wouldn't even know where he was.

But she didn't want Andy to be alone. And she had to admit, his goals were her goals too. She had to support this mission.

"You can trust Chris," she told him. "He's smart and nice and brave. Take him with you."

"You'll be the boss," Chris told Andy. "I'll take orders from you."

"Okay," Andy said. "You're on."

Amy sat down on the sofa next to Eric. Waves of sadness washed over her. Eric put his good arm around her shoulders. She looked up at him through eyes misty with tears.

"You've still got me," he said. "I'll be here for you."

She smiled. She looked at Andy, and then she looked at Chris. They were blurry, but she could see that their eyes were as full of tears as her own.

Andy spoke gruffly. "Let's go, Chris."

"Okay."

At that moment, the doorbell rang. Chris hurried to the window and looked out. He seemed concerned by what he saw out there. "Hey, boss . . ."

"What?" Andy asked sharply.

"Can we have some pizza first? You can't start a quest for world survival on an empty stomach."

"Good point," Andy said. "I think we're going to get along just fine."

They grinned at each other. Amy smiled too. She would just have to learn to get along without them.